OUR LIVES ARE FAIRY TALES

Natacha Pavlov

The Spirit gives life; the flesh counts for nothing.
—Jesus (John 6:63)

Why wouldn't you want your life to be like a fairy tale?
(Dream #5 – May 25th, 2013)

CONTENTS

JUDAEAN MEMORIES

St. Gerasimos / Deir Hajla Monastery, West Bank

Gradually, the priest came to his senses. The darkness didn't intimidate him; almost instantly his eyes adjusted as he lay there, enjoying the gentle yet powerful stillness that filled him. He'd been awake a few minutes already, his body attuned to an early rising. He glanced at the table next to his bed, the drawer beckoning to him. A faint smile grew upon his lips as he gripped the cross at his neck.

Everywhere, I feel you everywhere, he repeated to himself.

By the time the bell had sounded off—the way it did every day before dawn—he'd already changed into his long, black Greek-style *riassa*, and had lightly passed a comb through his thick black hair. A faint glow emitted through his room's small square window, barely enough light for untrained eyes. But it was all he needed, for he knew his quarters too well to necessitate lighting a candle.

Moments later, he stepped outside, shutting the door quietly behind him. The warm, dry air grazed his skin as he immersed himself in the early morning greyness of the desert. He walked with determination at an even pace, his leather sandals stepping so lightly upon the gravel that they barely made a sound. His beloved routine: rising early before the sunrise, praying and thinking in silence in this remote area with the beautiful surrounding hills as his other, ever faithful companions. Each day a new beginning, despite his life's daily repetitiveness. Yet he was luckiest of all: a life with prayer and community alongside his faithful, loving brothers, and catering to their few animals, of which he was the main source. He smiled at the nearby sound of rotund sand partridges calling softly to each other. Such were the simple joys that made for his perfect life.

He sighed. As usual, there'd also be visitors later, just as there were every day: people of all backgrounds coming to absorb some Holy Land history, some believers, some not. But he generally didn't mingle with them, preferring instead to observe and maintain a low profile. A safe distance—one of the reasons he'd been drawn to this very location.

At last he stood still, his body facing in the direction of the mountains in the distance. That was it: the ideal place that was just right and carried a sense of comfort and purpose. It also felt... familiar somehow. He'd seen many beautiful places—as indeed he found God's beauty to be present everywhere—but the thought of the nearby Qumran Caves and the Dead Sea Scrolls had always arrested him. A feeling like reassurance overcame him. The speculations were many, but he always loved to think of the Son of Man as having come close to them, perhaps even walked in them. Yet, he also knew that the miracles and beauty of nature were enough to fill his heart with awe—and surely a humbling sign of God's presence.

He closed his eyes and prayed silently, breathing deeply, following the method his parents had instilled in him as a child growing up in Crete. He was a generally tranquil man—how can one be anything less when thus absorbed in the all-encompassing source of serene, patient love?—but once more he sensed the growing burst of energy deep inside him. So, so *alive*. It was there in varying intensities on different days, and that morning it was distinctly powerful; something he'd swear had been slowly but surely blossoming within him the past few days. That feeling that filled him up and possessed him completely—*that* was what made it all worth it. He could have no fears, no worries, no anger, no regrets, no sadness in the presence of such a sentiment. And such was the source of his joy at the thought of being able to live another day to worship his Creator.

Each day is a new day, he thought. *How old am I? No, rather: how new am I!* he pondered with gratefulness.

Jerusalem

There was something about looking at so much vastness that filled my vision with endless images. Empty—one thing this place had never been and couldn't possibly ever be, no matter its deserted appearance. The warm air enveloped my face, blanketing my whole body with its saltiness. My right arm extended out the window, the thick air almost palpable in my hand, as the car steadily sped along. I liked that tingling feeling of grasping the elusive wind, and my eyes closed as I let myself get lost in the moment. I'd almost lost all sensation of my hand, flailing freely in the wind, when I felt a growing warm, hot, then burning sensation on my finger. Capitulating to the conquering heat, I retreated my hand back inside and pulled off the searing gold ring with amethyst stone from my finger. The ancient ring: the one item I'd worn ever since I could remember. It'd always given me a sense of reassurance and stability, and removing it felt like I would've broken some kind of promise. So there it faithfully remained.

The familiar Arabic lyrics to Amr Diab's famous "Noor El Ain" blared from the radio—Jabra, the driver, having turned up the volume—and I glimpsed the rosary wrapped around his rearview mirror gently swinging as I endeavored to cool down my piece of jewelry. I'd always found the tune cheerful and uplifting, and I couldn't help but smile as I heard the driver faintly sing along, as if holding himself back from full passionate public display of emotion.

The chorus repeated, and the lyrics had never struck me as romantic as they did right then. Could someone love another through their imagination? Could thought be enough to keep love alive? And yet, how to decipher love's true source? Is a person truly loved or is it rather their Creator who is? How to determine the difference? Such probing concepts had always interested me, but given our strange human natures, it seemed they didn't always apply to the complexities of love.

Shifting in my seat, I noted 12:33 p.m. on the green-numbered clock display, aware we were approaching our destination. The excursion hadn't been planned, but I'd woken up that day feeling peculiar, even frustrated, like something was calling out to me from *somewhere*. I'd suddenly had the urge to get away; away from the tension of Jerusalem and be somewhere else, like out into the expansive, peaceful desert. A month in Jerusalem had attuned me to different energies, and I found myself repeatedly drawn to that area. I figured it must be the urge to return home—that ephemeral and yet real place—and then it came to me that I should do this last thing before I left. But the irony of that feeling was not lost on me. Why did I keep coming here? Why that constant habit: romanticizing the place while away, wanting to return, and once back almost immediately questioning my decision. Did I never learn? Maybe that was just one of the side effects of traveling—those spontaneous rollercoaster emotions, that after all this time still caught me off guard—but still I tried to decipher the peculiar mix of contemplative, frustrated, and amusing effect it had on me.

A joy overcame me then, and I smiled: captivated by the sight, I could hardly question my visit. The landscapes surrounding the Dead Sea had fascinated me ever since I'd first laid eyes on them: I loved the caves and my attraction to them bordered on the obsessive. Silly, it seemed; how one could feel so strongly about a place they technically hardly knew. I always joked that I would run away and live in them if I could... but I wasn't sure I was entirely bluffing. There, somehow, the tension dissipated, and I'd felt at peace. The peace I'd wanted to feel all throughout that land but which seemed to make itself known when one least expected it. I'd felt similarly before, but never to the extent I felt there. And then, I realized that as much as I'd enjoyed many places in the area—like covering myself in mud and floating in the salty Dead Sea, visiting the Saint George monastery and the Mount of Temptation—there was one more I had yet to explore.

As the car forged ahead, the scenery maintained its constant simplicity—two lane road, electric poles, gravel-filled, treeless patches of land, faraway dusty hills—so that I could see the unobstructed path unfolding straight ahead of us. On the opposing left side of the highway were modest Palestinian stands offering fruits and trinkets. I spotted a camel: tall, silent, very still. I laughed at the sight of this fake effigy, surely meant to amuse tourists, until I saw it lift one of its legs. I loved being reminded that every place had potential for surprises, and some would particularly expect them in that land. The perpetual imagery and afternoon warmth fueled a feeling of ease and relaxation. Rocked by the motion of the car, drowsiness overcame me.

It's been long, so long, I heard a man say.

I know, I replied.

I jilted awake, just as the car made a slowed turn off the road, entering a parking area with cars and travel buses, indicating the place already had some visitors. At last, we'd reached our destination. I came to my senses, resolving to snap out of my brief, hazy reverie as I put my ring back on and wrapped my satchel and camera around my shoulder. I stepped out as the serene setting revealed nearby hills in the midst of which stood the non-imposing, limestone monastery of Saint Gerasimos.

Smiling, Jabra nodded to me then drifted to some familiar faces, where he'd patiently await the end of my visit. I entered the monastery from the west side, and stepped into a quaint stone courtyard embellished with several plants and numerous ancient stone tools. Decorations graced the entrance. Nestled between the blue Greek flag and red Orthodox Church flag was a painting of Saint Gerasimos, the fingers of his right hand curved in a sign of blessing to visitors. Glimpsing Jabra's approving smile once more, I slipped through the narrow entrance.

I arrived at a small courtyard, with a well at the center on which stood a crucifix and a painting of Saint Gerasimos and the lion. Large, red-potted plants were placed on each side, whose tall green leaves contrasted the structure's orange-tinged stones. The sculpture of a lion's head located on the ground nearby also caught my eye. The legend told that Gerasimos had encountered the lion by the nearby Jordan River, where the creature lay in pain caused by a thorn in its paw. The Abbot helped the lion and it eventually became part of the community. Whether factual or metaphorical, I'd always been fascinated by stories of animals and humans bonding in unexpected, often miraculous ways.

It was then that I noticed how quiet it was, so that for a moment it was as though I was the only visitor. Moments later, I heard echoes of voices—sounds like Greek, Russian, English, maybe French—that confirmed visitors' presence in the vicinity. As the courtyard lit up with sunlight, I wondered how nice and peaceful it must be to dwell there. I lingered for a bit, observing and leisurely taking pictures.

Ready to explore the rooms inside the building, I turned, meaning to go up the stairs to explore the second floor when I was suddenly faced with a massive multi-colored rooster. With its white-feathered body, cream-colored head and black tail feathers, the creature made a majestic sight. Amused by the unexpected appearance, I slowly approached it, not wanting to startle it, and it eyed me as though used to such speculation. Thus acquainted and passage granted, I smiled at the thought that the colorful bird's companions, wherever they were, likely served the noble purpose of providing eggs to the monastery's humble residents.

At the top of the stairs was a cloister to my left lined with wooden doors—likely the priests' rooms. I glimpsed a small image of the Virgin Mary next to one of Jesus secured on the door by a small wooden cross. The simplicity of the gesture touched me, bringing to mind the Christian Orthodox tradition of placing importance on religious icons.

I turned to the right and entered a small, white brick-walled chapel. I noted the narthex's arched ceilings, from which hung chandeliers, a painting of its patron saint, and white candles for sale. I loved its aura of peace and quiet and continued to the right, proceeding into the main church area.

Typical of Orthodox churches, the altar wall stood, creating a mysterious, metaphorical separation between the hidden altar and the visitors' hall area. The icons depicted Mary and Jesus, scenes of Jesus's life, and various saints clad in predominantly blue and gold hues—the gold triggering images of God's fiery, all-consuming love. A few modest benches were placed throughout; the aged wood making me wonder how many others had sat on them throughout the years.

And perhaps also how many hadn't. I recalled that Saint Gerasimos had attended the Council of Chalcedon in 451 AD; that most fateful of early Christian events that sealed the split between the Chalcedonian and Monophysite definitions of the divine nature and person of Jesus. Did these aims—obsessing over words to describe His single nature, as the Monophysites said, or dual nature in one, as the Chalcedonians claimed—really mean to help us become better Christians, or rather to deepen our divisions? Were these inseparable? Could there not be just one congregation, allied in the worship of Jesus, regardless of perceived "correct" definitions?

Facing the altar, I noted more frescoes in adjacent columns. What had the Crusaders thought when they'd seen them? Had they been touched, unable to destroy such ancient art that had stood the test of time? Mesmerized by the colors and details, I examined the old walls, their cracks extending from side to side testifying to their endurance. I questioned how close they were to the authentic drawings. Can art truly be conserved to such a degree? Or is it meant to change with time, much as its own surroundings do?

My gaze fell upon the geometrical patterns at my feet. I knelt down and my fingers traced the small ancient squares in faded white, orange, and navy blue hues. Images of artists at work upon these mosaics instantly came to mind, and a sense of renewed respect and awe for the timeless work swept over me.

In a way, I thought this monastery east of Jericho felt somewhat different from the churches I'd seen in Jerusalem. Perhaps it was the isolation that made the place feel older. Despite the tourists it drew, it would probably never be as crowded or fought over as the Holy Sepulchre—presumed site of the Crucifixion—or the birthplace of Jesus in Bethlehem's Church of the Nativity. Yet how does one determine when a place is holy? What makes it holy? Is the importance of a place judged by how many visitors it draws? Deir Hajla was indeed quieter, emptier, in a way... and what if that was the very thing that made it retain its authenticity? For how could throngs of people repeatedly pass through a place without altering it somehow? A million thoughts raced through my mind, each one harder to answer than its precedent.

And there was more, for the caves were nearby. These limestone rocky mountains I'd felt so drawn to—the memory I most treasured from my first time driving by the Dead Sea caves. I'd stretched out my arms from the window, waving to the caves as though I hadn't seen them in ages, practically wishing I could grasp them in their entirety in my arms in a warm embrace. It'd felt surreal seeing them in all their glory, their ragged cliffs more affected by nature than by man. And what of the random nooks here and there; perfectly sized openings in the wall that would instantly beg the question: had one of its residents done it? Scenes would play out in my mind—men and women dressed in biblical clothing, adhering to their strict Essene lifestyle removed from the outside, spiritually-divided society. The caves, so emblematic of nature, must've differentiated them from everyone else. Surely people had to be affected by their surroundings, particularly when it consists of so much nature. And yet, just being able to carve out a niche somewhere in the world—is that not happiness enough? Love, gratitude: that's what it must've felt like. Reassured and confident to forge on, no matter the circumstances, knowing and feeling safe in the midst of a natural fortress.

Thus absorbed, my body almost unconsciously curled over the mosaic with my camera in hand, as in a trance, snapping photos from various angles. My camera already counted a collection of churches taken throughout the country, and I wouldn't miss this opportunity to add yet another to my series of Holy Land Christian sites.

Onwards, I wandered until I reached the first room of the crypt. I stepped into the entrance hall, where low arched ceilings were painted in light sky and royal blue shades. There were more sets of biblical paintings in gold frames hung throughout the room, by now a familiar sight. Continuing straight ahead, at last I came upon the back wall, the glare no longer obstructing its detailed representation. I realized I'd never seen such a depiction of one of the most common Christian scenes. Adorned with a jeweled crown and red cloak, the Virgin Mary breastfed the Holy infant Jesus wrapped in white. I recalled someone mentioning that Joseph, Mary and the Child had hidden in a nearby cave as they'd fled to Egypt from Herod's wrathful decree, ordering the execution of all young male children two years old and under, seeking to eradicate the prophesied threat to his throne. Had they indeed passed through that place? And how fascinating that somehow this was the place that came to commemorate it.

While I felt that biblical passages always had a way of sounding so extraordinary, it was easy to forget that they also involved simpler scenes of daily life. The natural image of a mother breastfeeding her child—holy though He is—brought a sense of authenticity and simplicity to this narrative that I'd seldom encountered before. The dichotomy of divine and human combined in one suddenly felt more relatable than ever.

After committing the image to memory and capturing several photos, I proceeded to the second room of the crypt. I beheld another small similar room with sky blue walls whose peeling paint revealed the grey-white limestone underneath. Shifting my gaze, I was then struck by the presence of wooden cabinets filled with bones. It instantly dawned on me that I'd never seen human bones in real life, much less so many of them gathered in a pile, unburied. I had the growing uneasy feeling in the pit of my stomach that these should be in the ground. Just the sight of them in such a state made it look *wrong*—messy, unidentified, so *exposed*—fueling the sad sense of incompletion.

For dust you are and to dust you will return, Genesis 3:19 echoed in my thoughts.

The discovery that they were remains from the Persian Massacre of 614 AD and the great earthquake of 1897 did little to ease my discomfort over their state—perhaps, awkwardly, it only reinforced it. I said a prayer to ease my malaise, wanting to depart the room with a sense of peace. My exploration of the second floor completed, I bid a silent adieu to the place as I enjoyed the last moments of coolness the cave-like rooms provided.

I traced my steps back down to the courtyard, where the protruding sun rays instantly wrapped me up in a warm embrace. I noted the souvenir and gift area and wandered over to browse, curious to see the kinds of gifts and trinkets I would find before the throng of tourists surfaced. A few tables were laid out, covered in Greek Orthodox holy objects: Orthodox prayer rope bracelets, hematite bracelets with little pictures of biblical scenes and Orthodox saints, olive wood rosaries, Orthodox icons of the Virgin and child Jesus, books on Saint Gerasimos. I smiled, reflecting on the modest prices, which would've easily doubled and tripled in Jerusalem's Old City. It was just another reminder of how some central locations would always take advantage of their favored space.

Contemplating the various items, I suddenly had the impression of being watched. Yet how could I justify such a feeling in this place? A ruffling at my feet made me shift and look down to see a black Terrier eager for some attention. I knelt down to pet his belly and detected a sandy film on his thick coat that betrayed his fondness for rolling in the dirt. Moments later, I stood up, brushing the dirt off my hands. It was then that I saw a priest standing a few feet away, quietly staring at me. I was caught off guard, for I hadn't heard him approach and I'd believed myself to be alone with the dog in the courtyard.

He was tall, of robust build, and wore a long black tunic with a wooden cross that hung low on his chest. His hair was thick and black, and was neatly gathered behind him in a ponytail. His piercing green eyes peered at me from under dark eyebrows, his full lips outlined by a short beard. I sensed an intensity about him, and I was both relieved and unsettled by his gaze that made me feel somehow utterly exposed. As the silence lingered, I felt overcome, a brewing shyness in me causing me to look away and avoid his mute, intent stare. My finger felt violently itchy—I was suddenly aware and bothered by the moisture caused by my heavy metallic ring—but I kept my hand behind me, not wanting to reveal any sign of agitation. He didn't say a word, and I don't know why I didn't expect him to. Somehow it seemed silence was the only exchange needed.

There was a bustle as tourists came around the corner, their presence dissipating the stillness with their lively chatter. He made as if to step back, and I thought I glimpsed a faint smile on his lips as I went back to shuffling through gifts. My satchel and camera now feeling like weights on me, I felt nervous, unable to really focus, as I looked at objects without really seeing them. Decisions, decisions: what to buy? At that moment, that felt like the least of my concerns.

As I continued perusing, I noticed the priest from the corner of my eye, lingering in a hallway to my right. He'd grabbed a chair and lowered himself ever so slowly onto it, as if careful not to miss any movement I made. He sat motionless, observing me. I felt torn; partially wanting to acknowledge him and maybe even speak to him, yet unsure about what to say. But strangest of all: why did I inexplicably feel connected to this man, and him apparently to me? Something like being a teenager again, that feeling like... butterflies in my stomach. But that made no sense, and my frustration started bordering on anger. My thoughts raced, tension built, until at last my resolve caved. I looked in his direction and our eyes met modestly, and his face now wore a transfixed, almost grievous expression. Instantly I was filled with the urge to comfort him—but my conflicted state held me back. I don't know what I'd expected from the day, aside from one last chance of sightseeing and memories, but suddenly it occurred to me that he somehow had something to do with it.

What were the odds that we'd see each other on this day? I hadn't planned the visit, and surely with his work and the other priests and visitors around, it seemed likely we could've easily missed each other. I would've walked away with good memories, a series of lovely pictures of this place,

even if they were mere ghosts of the actual experience. The sudden realization that he wouldn't be in any of these images instantly struck at
my heart, and I felt a deep, overwhelming sadness. No pictures, no *proof*.
Just an encounter I'd ingrain in my memory and somehow expect it not
to fade away. And yet, that sensation of sadness dissipated as quickly as it
came. As a wave of warm acceptance washed over me, I gave him a gentle,
understanding smile. I didn't wait to see his reaction for I'd looked away,
my vision having blurred as tears threatened to overflow.

As I grew increasingly emotional, I gathered my trinkets and paid, realizing that my visit had reached its end. A feeling of bitter-sweetness crept up
again, so I cast one more glance where he sat, as if he might understand. But
the limestone walls revealed only a quiet, empty hall and chair. Immobile,
I stood staring at the vacant seat, realizing yet again that I hadn't felt him
leave. I thought I'd imagined the faint flutter I saw springing up from
the chair; an object's sudden movement. I kept staring, as though waiting
would reveal the nature of the mystery. I hadn't realized that I'd walked over
to the chair, until I stood in front of it and beheld a small leather-bound
book with open, silky pages fluttering to and fro in the thick summer
breeze. Amidst the flickering text of the Greek language I couldn't read,
I caught familiar words. Pinning down the fragile pages to confirm my
impression, my eyes locked in on the letters.

Άγγελος και Αικατερίνη

Next to them was a detailed sketch of a ring with a unique, ancient style,
decorated with a purple stone. So lifelike—reflecting that the undeniably
skilled artist had spent countless hours in its contemplation, creating the
exact depiction of this prized ring—a ring I knew all too well.

Something in me cracked: a sob caught in my throat as my hand flew to
my mouth to conceal my violent reaction. Pulling away, I rushed through
the entrance's archway, concealing my face as I looked down. I paced to the
parked car where Jabra sat, his timely awareness of my fast approach setting
the engine ablaze. I threw myself into the faded blue leather backseats.

The feeling overpowered me, an overwhelming impression that I needed
to get away; not wanting anyone, least of all *him* to see me start crying.
Crying, weeping, for reasons I wasn't sure of but in some ways felt all too
familiar. Sadness enveloped me; a lifetime of memories and feelings rushing
at me as the tears poured down my face, dripping onto my hands and

lap. Wringing my hands, I felt the gold band around my finger moistened by my salty tears, as I slipped it off with a quick motion. I looked at the stone—that final moment before confirmation. But I knew it; I had to face it. I could no longer deny the truth of something I'd sought for so long. I held the ring like a worry stone—the one ring I'd always owned, and which was so old no one in my family was sure of its origin, only that it'd been passed on. The story I'd been told: that this was a ring specifically meant for me, that tied me to The One who loved me greatly. As always; bits and pieces of stories retained, leaving one to go along and piece it altogether themselves. As I looked into the ring's inner band, the way I had done countless times, I finally understood who the engraved names belonged to.

Άγγελος και Αικατερίνη
Angelos and Aikaterine
It felt so familiar—this act of leaving behind something you love for reasons that made sense, for a million that didn't. The circumstances all wrong; did it always have to be this hard? And who could say which way was best, when one realizes that love never truly stops, but remains as if locked away in a box until the right time makes it unlock, releasing it all over again?

Caught in the whirlwind of pain and love, the car's noisy engine felt like a protective shroud; its metallic chaos drowning out my gut-wrenching wailing sorrow.

I was sure: I'd never cried this hard in my life. At least not in this one. As a flow of long forgotten memories resurfaced in my mind, I recalled the lifetime in which I'd known him. The one when our destinies had been linked, and yet I was forced to make a choice that would preserve our lives instead of risk it all in the name of... love. So, so long ago, but the pain of it manifested itself all over again, tears streaming endlessly as I doubled over to clutch the deep pain in my stomach. How willing we are to die for it, but what about life? I wanted to *live*. And live I did: in misery for being away from him, but neither could I ever say that I'd regretted my choice.

Love.

His love... does not *die*. Death is the very anti-thesis of the word, for His love is life and therefore cannot be death. I learned it the hard way but despite all of it, it never lost its inherent sweetness; its essence forever pure. I've always missed him and have often longed for him, looked for him, wondered who *he* was; not even entirely sure who I was searching for. And yet, I've learned to replace that void with something much greater: the One who died in this land two thousand years ago, the one who first brought us together in infinite ways. How many times did it happen? How many lifetimes did I have—or not have—with him? Would the outcome ever change?

I know nothing—*nothing*. That is why I submit, and though I do not understand all of life's mysteries, I am satisfied. They're not *logical*: the things of the heart hardly ever are. They operate by a different law, and who am I to go against it? And so I live, with my only hope being that with every opportunity I somehow become better, create some moments of happiness, cause a little less pain—for both others and myself.

As the torrent of my tears somewhat subsided, the motion of the car rocked my body in a comforting, bittersweet embrace. Wiping my tears away, I sought to capture one last image. Peering through the rear windshield, I discerned outlines amidst the trail of dirt the speeding vehicle left in its wake. The sun beamed upon the fading church structure, the red dome and its neighboring metallic-domed roof like fiery, glinting stars as they diminished on the horizon.

Why do I keep coming back here, I've asked myself so many times, aware it wouldn't be the last time. And I realized that sometimes, just knowing it's there—that that love exists somewhere, no matter where, in the world—can be enough.

He'd realized he'd let slip his Bible, and for a minute panicked, wondering where had it gone? But then he caught himself—in that small monastery nothing ever got lost. He'd quickly retraced his steps and arrived in time to see her near the chair, absorbed in one of the pages. Smiling, he resolved he would finally speak to her, when she suddenly appeared distraught and quickly left. By the time he arrived and held his Bible, her faint but distinct fingerprints were still on the page with the sketched ring—the final confirmation. He held it open, pressed to his heart as he prayed, and it was a while before he left the site.

Yes, things were always found... and most importantly, so were people. He'd found himself there too, as had the other priests, but he could never forget that tugging at his heart that would make itself known from time to time. Curious thing it is; when you feel a kind of deep sadness, longing for something, only to find a warm kind of forgiving, all-encompassing love—a different love, of course—wrapping you up in its embrace. He would always feel that longing, he suspected, but he also knew that one can never feel alone when in the presence of Christ, the Anointed One. And it wasn't a matter of choosing—perhaps the greatest challenge was uniting these two forms of love, out of which to create something as unique as the varieties of life on this earth.

Leaning over the bed, he reached for the small cupboard next to him and opened the drawer. His hand found the ring, and traced over the etched names on its inner surface.

Ἄγγελος και Αικατερίνη

Angelos and Aikaterine

He brought the ancient gold ring closer to his eyes, more out of habit than of need to study it. Yet despite having memorized all its details, it always felt as if he was looking at it for the first time. The same powerful feelings surfaced, fueling a mixed feeling of helplessness and elated invincibility.

He'd watched her as she moved, had examined the traits; all the ways in which she still seemed and felt so *familiar*. But things were never entirely the same—one cannot be reborn and repeat the journey in exactly the same way. Growth: the way our Lord has intended but, always, provided the free will is receptive.

He'd seen her hand draw quickly to her side, but not fast enough for the sun to conceal the bright purple stone adorning her finger. There was no mistaking: it was the match to his own ring he now held, and had possessed all his life, passed on across generations.

A gold ring with an amethyst stone, gifted to his beloved.

A lifetime ago.

He closed his eyes and smiled, overcome with emotion. *Thank you my Lord, thank you for today*, he prayed, tears streaming down his face. *All in Your divine timing.* [1]

---

1. *Semi-finalist for Ruminate Magazine's Fall 2014 William Van Dyke Short Story Prize. As an early short story, it was welcomed inspiration to keep writing, as I was also in the early stages of researching and writing my sixth century novel Jayida, the work that first made me want to write historical fiction.*

THE CRUSADER

Jerusalem, Fall 1099 AD

There's a heaviness on my chest that sometimes I think will never leave.

I don't think that I want it to: I relish that consuming pressure that fills me, the crush of metal that I push back against, perpetually constraining, reminding me of my physical limits. Yet always, I'll feel that boundless energy resurface from somewhere deep within, entwined amidst my pulsating, meaty organs—teasing me that it's an illusion. I squeeze, and the coldness feels too thin in my fist now, and I look down, ease up on my butter knife grip: I'm simply slicing some herring.

There's a familiar chorus, and I don't need to look to know that the same movie is replaying, filling the space with distinct roaring echoes: clashing swords, tormented cries, gushing blood and organs, writhing villains and heroes. There's no time to ask which one I am when trying to survive—this much I know—but at some point life comes full circle and you look back at yourself, and then there's no more running away. Because somehow you know they can't all be correct, and the fact is you fit in somewhere.

It's Him who put that explosive fighting survival in me, and being Christ's and Abraham's seed, and therefore heir according to the promise, I could never fully separate myself from the Holy Land, the land where He incarnated, to be cruelly crucified in Jerusalem. He knew the fullness of our ugliness and—the part that hurts most—that's precisely why He did it.

Even after all this time, I contemplate how to humble myself to that level, and in His eternal, patient grace, I keep learning. No blood of mine is enough to repay that sacrifice, but I'm vain enough to think I often feel Him nearby. I need no motivation for loyalty other than the blessed feeling that filled me when told the holy stories as a young boy, and by now I know I'll never shake what pushed me to such a journey so long ago—the best tormenting reward of all. I have many faults but my proudest lesson has been—and remains—that when I hear God's call, it's my duty to answer.

By all standards I had everything: dwelling in the Flemish coastal village of Leffinge with doting parents; my long days spent in Oostende learning my father's fisherman trade leaving me as smelly as happily exhausted. My kind, selfless *mam* had such a skilled hand that some of her clothmaking even came to grace our local church. As word spread, a few times we even traveled as far as Lille to sell at the markets, and with the Lord's blessing, in time our earnings even granted me some education from the monks.

While everything seemed set for me, it's not out of ungratefulness when I say that it was little consolation for my restless soul. Where *was* that mission to make me forget myself and my own selfish wants—this hell tearing at me, questioning my very purpose and right to live! The faint cry seized me in the dark: that others had it much worse was something I was sensitive to, and knew could befall us at any moment, too. So what was I searching for? I kept it to myself that sometimes a part of me wanted to leave everything before I lost it all.

Then, with the might of the seraphim it came.

The news gripped me, as much for its vileness as for its timely answer to my heart's longing—wilder than anything I could've imagined. A dark premonition filled me, confirming unspoken fears: the world as we knew it was now on the brink of collapse. That much was evident from the plea of far-dwelling Emperor Alexius Comnenus, whose eastern empire sacked by Seljuk barbarians was at last answered by our good Pope Urban's moving speech. Like wildfire it spread, igniting all hearts for the proper cause: the Holy Land to be rightfully restored into faithful Christian hands, and mending the recent rift with Emperor Alexius's Eastern Orthodox Church.

What had once been wonderful, cryptic words heard at Sunday masses, whose meaning I, a mere mortal, could never fully decipher, gathered like a triumphant storm in my soul, ready to unfurl in worthy battle. Here was the chance to restore us all to the One true church; the ultimate test of my faith and for the first time in my life I had no shred of hesitation. Its power and purpose seized me, because I needed no Pope's proclamation that anyone who did it for devotion alone would be free from penance. I would never say it aloud that such a thing sounded vain, even for a Pope, but I took added comfort in that decree.

Eager to make my parents, as much as Him, proud, after mass I informed them of my intent to join the expedition. I was still a healthy, unmarried man with my life ahead of me, and though I'd noticed a few potential matches I could eventually start a life with, none so far had claimed my heart. As such I was unattached, and my father's good name promptly allowed me to secure my place as infantryman in the army of Robert II, Count of Flanders.

Though I initially considered rejoining Peter the Hermit and his recruits, fast gathering at Amiens, I wanted to be guided by experienced leaders and knights. My faith was not so blind as to make me ignore the realities of our undertaking, and though I admired ardent displays of faith, the likes of which many of us had never witnessed, I respected and understood the necessity for skilled leadership.

My heart blazing like the summer sun lighting the gold cross potent necklace on my chest, we departed Robert of Flanders's castle at Lille, leaving his wife Clementia as regent in his absence.

Our glorious gathering steadily grew as we rejoined the retinues of Robert of Normandy, Stephen of Blois, Hugh of Vermandois and Raymond of Toulouse. Such was the procession of the Princes' Crusade, and soon we heard that we even had Lusignan nobles among us, whose impressive fortified castle in Poitou fast generated awed respect.

We journeyed southeast through France and the Kingdom of Italy, with Bohemond of Taranto and his camp joining us to converge with Godfrey of Bouillon—that proud descendant of Charlemagne—in Constantinople. Ecstatic with Bishop Adhemar of Le Puy's presence and sermons to accompany us, we grew closer to Jerusalem with every dedicated onward step.

Deus vult! Deus vult!—such was the rhythm of our march, the echoing chants cloaking us like indestructible holy armor.

There was also Aldric; that name that quickly came to be known throughout our camp. He was what every man wished to be: young, strong, handsome, and of noble extract that went back generations along with his wealthy inheritance. Though it initially made some reluctant of him, he lost no time in offering motivation when men's exhaustion dulled their spirits. Vain, heartless nobles were plenty, but so were noblemen worthy of their rank.

Despite my cautious reservation, gradually an unspoken bond formed between us that seemed to diminish our individual differences and unite us in our sacred higher mission. Perhaps it was the fire gatherings, drawing stories and spirits out of us that made us forget ourselves, while some flattered themselves as potential *trouvères* in training. It helped that Aldric had a way of making those around him feel like they were in the presence of something great, and that they'd been chosen to witness it. And though at times I found it naively extreme and unnecessary, I took the loyalty I saw develop to Aldric as a sign of commendable trust that should enhance our mission.

I thought I'd glimpsed him suppress a wince, when in Constantinople Emperor Alexius Comnenus demanded the territories be given back to them in glory of their Orthodox faith. Though I cared not for spoils, I understood the sting of doing the hard work only for its rewards to be granted to another. But we couldn't forget our sacred assignment that belongs to all those who bravely fight for it, and the agreements were made.

We left Constantinople, forging past our predecessors' disastrous defeat at Civetot, and I thanked the Lord for having kept me from going along with Peter the Hermit and his followers. But nothing, we soon started to suspect, would be easily won. We'd entered the belly of the beast; the heat searing us as we trudged the difficult terrain and fended off hit-and-run attacks from savage Saracens. The heaviness clung to us, adding endless weight to my cherished, and envied, mail hauberk as it protected me at every moment. But despite our challenges we forged through victories at Nicaea, Dorylaeum, and Heraclea, bolstering our wavering confidence as much as Bishop Adhemar's constant inspiring sermons.

Eager to push on, our camps split up, with our main army advancing through Cappadocia, whose pointy rock formations like strange, ancient impaling posts eerily contrasted the welcoming residing Armenians. But the journey went on and soon, tense, long shadows consumed us as our baggage animals and supplies dwindled, making increasingly grotesque images of our darkened, sunken faces. I prayed like never before to forget my hunger, hoping that Baldwin and Tancred's wanderings south added to our cause's success.

In time I came to feel Aldric before I saw him, drawing closer to me in a way that both flattered and discomforted me. His hot breath grazed my neck, hovering.

"Narduin, Narduin. With that glorious, well-concealed long mane of dark hair and deep-set features, you might almost blend in," he purred one day as we set camp near Antioch. "All the same, I'll have to enoble you for your bravery at our return."

His gaze lingered and I refrained from saying that I only looked for that from our Savior, though I imagined he suspected it. Worse yet, there was something unpleasant, unnatural in the way he said my name. I chuckled and looked away, eager to shake off the strange feeling creeping over me even as I gave thanks to the Holy Ghost for alerting me. I noted his playful air, and thankfully he said no more of it.

In any journey the camaraderie and relations will shift at some point, because the initial elation never lasts, or not as long as you'd want it to. While there was too much raging in my soul to notice everything happening around me, I noticed that Aldric had changed since we'd left, filling me with a reluctance I couldn't explain. We were all facing challenges in our own way, and with his entourage of admirers I was inclined to stay away, if only to process everything in the little quiet solitude I could get amidst an increasingly agitated camp. I concluded that his initial demeanor was a façade, and this offer to enoble me reeked of the kind that always had to remind others of their superiority, and worse, nearly demanding gratitude for being considered—as if I'd even asked for it. Despite the tempting honor, I was not one so easily seduced, even at my young age.

Perhaps he steered clear of me because eventually everyone knew. The late night grunts, the lowered gazes and pervading, tense silences—reordering the ranks amongst men, because the fact is they're always there. The served and the servants, and the question becomes: how much of each do you do; when do the scales tip? Challenges: that's what we knew this journey would bring, the testing of our fleshly urges not least among them.

There's something about need—or is it greed—that feeds the beast in us. But even beasts recognize their limits. And though I tried not to pass judgment, whatever bonds—if bonds they were—that had formed among some others were not the kind I'd ever partake in. I already recoiled at the thought of taking an unwilling woman, and though some might consider me less of a man for it, I did not answer to them nor was I one to back away from proving my manhood if anyone dared try to test me for it. Though Pope Urban's decree of absolution and remission of sins were never far from my thoughts, the more time passed the more I questioned if, given our holy mission, we'd truly be pardoned or, on the contrary, punished more severely for our transgressions.

My strength was only possible by His words, for what did all the world mean, when only one destination mattered? I couldn't be the only one with such thoughts, but even if I was, I tried to give thanks that I would not be swayed. I vowed that I would bear my hardships as He did, gladly suffering and without complaint. But of all the times in my life, I would not, could not, lie to myself either, when He—the only one I couldn't hide from—watched at every moment. Something was changing in me, too; softening my heart even as it hardened in endless subtle, nearly imperceptible ways.

The Lord always has and always will know, but confession is a kind of release of the burden weighing on your soul. For whatever heavenly visions I had of Jerusalem only declined from the moment we arrived at Antioch. Such a cruel irony to be so close yet feel so far from our goal.

With the citadel looking down on us from its thousand-foot high mountain, we had no choice but to camp outside its walls. The days and nights stretched on, but I tried to make the best of it, learning useful words of Arabic and Greek for when we at last reached the Holy City.

Then, the brutal blistering winter set in, and with food lacking once again, desertion and death rose. Whispers shivered down my spine. I kept them at bay but they were there, sure as you feel a ghostly presence without needing to see it.

One man, then another, and another—vanished into the barren snowscapes.

Aldric cheerful again, offering me some cooked, seasoned meat, looking almost offended when I refused. "A soldier needs to keep his strength; he knows this," he shrugged to one of his admirers.

Fear, amplifying everything even as it diminished others. That's what hunger does: changes everything you see, tempts you to ask what life you could suck out of it. The scent of burning, roasting flesh. My organs gnawing on themselves, I almost wished I could allow myself the illusion that it was the same, but try as I might—I still shudder even to say it—I couldn't do it.

Oh, how easily you'll say you'd never do such a thing, but you can never know what you'll do until you're faced with it. Somehow, I vowed that I would eat my own flesh first before I ate another's—and how I begged the Lord to just end me before I could do either horrible thing.

But all was possible with His strength; I could disappoint the Deceiver and send him back to hell. So I foraged for grasses, truffles, any and everything, no matter how pointless if only to keep myself moving. I rationed the little water I had, as my body mass lightened and yet, endured.

Then, another miracle in our midst. A relic of the holy lance discovered, the comforting visions of saints and angels reviving our spirits as we charged at the enemy. That's the story that circulated, and for once even I didn't find Aldric's coy smile in poor taste. No piece of relic could ever encompass all I felt, but objects play their part, in clear and mysterious ways. Faith is always what pushes men to action. It's a miracle, too, that no one considered eating it.

If we shamefully vacillated, so did our leaders, when Stephen of Blois and Hugh of Vermandois left to return home, leaving Bohemond of Taranto to claim the Antioch citadel for himself. Then it was Bishop Adhemar of Le Puy's turn to leave us for his heavenly reward. Many envied him, and with his unifying presence gone, this time I knew Aldric's smile to be sincere, even satisfied.

The only path left was ahead, so we kept on and I fought—I pushed through it all, charging alongside our leader Robert II of Flanders, Aldric, and countless others, lost in a blazing fury that wasn't my doing and prayed would never be. The enemy that had once been so clear now blurred, merging with everything around me, making everyone turn on each other regardless of faith. It was endless brandishing and striking to protect myself, and there was pleasure in that, to see the engulfing flames and know that you were unscathed as everyone else fell. I had not come so far only to fail now!

But why did it feel so far from victory, so unlike what I'd envisioned? Worst of all was the consuming sense of not knowing what or who to trust—like a possessing force controlling my actions without my knowledge or permission. At night I stole away from the carnage of Ma'arrat al-Nu'man—the famine pushing some to feed on the flesh of Saracens—crumbling before what felt like the loss of my sanity, praying for my strength to last me at least until I finally set eyes on Jerusalem.

We swept through the Fatimid territory on our southern path to Jerusalem, finding little but poisoned wells, hacked trees and flocks driven away, adding to our desolation. Aldric seethed, and I wondered where he got the energy for such a feeling.

Finally, three years after my journey had begun, we trudged up a mountaintop and froze, stunned, as we finally beheld holy Jerusalem, crowned in its arid summer glow. Sharp cries resonated, arms lifted to heaven, and I fell to my knees, and even in my anguish I knew we weren't all shedding tears for the same reasons. Nothing was I'd expected—no unshakeable union among men as I'd longed for. Shallow, and maybe even complete lack of faith, our numbers drastically reduced—and yet something in me sprang up in immeasurable joy, too, like that was not the point nor for me to control, confirming it was not for nothing. To commemorate our arrival, we renamed the mountain Mons Gaudii, though I consigned to my memory its name of Dayr Shamwil and its nearby monastery.

Eager to beat the local Fatimid rulers to an imminent strike, we resolved to take the city by assault. Although we suffered a blowing initial defeat, it was not to last, when yet another miracle overtook us: echoes resounded of visions of Bishop of Adhemar, counseling us to fast and march barefoot around the city walls, sure to secure our victory like Joshua at the Battle of Jericho.

Then, Genoese mariners arrived at Jaffa, and with our drenched brows dripping in the summer heat, we wasted no time in using the ships' timber and foraging for more wood to build our siege towers. Raymond of Toulouse stationed to the south, while the rest of us positioned to the north with Godfrey of Bouillon, Robert of Flanders, Tancred, and Robert of Normandy. Before this, every task, though honorable and necessary stepping stones, still sometimes felt like a far-off dream, but now being in the city we'd fought so hard to reach filled us with unquenchable, supernatural strength.

Bolstered with the appearance of Peter the Hermit and ecstatic to praise our incarnated God, our entire gathering dutifully marched around the city in procession, ascending east up the Mount of Olives to finish with a blessed, overdue sermon. Emotional wrath seized me, because if the Saracens persecuted Christians and forbade their right to worship in their homeland ever since their invasion four centuries before, at last our arrival could help enact changes. At last, we had our final, glorious proof: if we succeeded, anything was possible.

As if sighting a burning bush in the pitch darkness, Godfrey suddenly moved us to a less defended section of the city walls. In the exploding blur the blaze unfurled, expanding time, and though I struck back only at those who attacked me, the rampage and carnage was complete. I saw Aldric morph into the bloodthirsty fighter I knew him to be: carefully concealed beneath, slashing indiscriminately at not just men, but women and children, Jew and Saracen. Even if I'd wanted to, he was so fast and merciless that even his followers, inspired by his example, could hardly keep up—wanting it all for himself. The suffocating smoke and overwhelming copper scent nearly choking me, I fought the sickness of such bloodshed violently seizing me. The deafening roar yielded to our shouting leaders claiming victory and brandishing bloody blades to the sky. So lacking, so different from what I'd envisioned, but no one could argue that the city was finally ours.

That night I set out on the pretext of perusing some of our surroundings, and though true, it was mostly to get away from their drunken celebrating. Even if many residents around us had already fled our rampaging capture, I had little fear for my life, mostly because I didn't even think of it. Let it be the Lord's will if I should die then—after all, I'd already fulfilled my vow of being part of this event, though I had no wish to sadden my parents. Many were already making their plans to return home, filled with a self-satisfied relief I tried not to envy, and I was reminded once more how different men can be. Conflict overtook me: I was in Jerusalem and I'd never felt so out of place, so unsure about my true destination.

I walked south in the dark, hoping I'd come upon something pure and special, like the monastery dedicated to Saint Mark I'd heard about. At length I entered a vast hilly area, whose dilapidated, flat-roofed homes added to my sad, empty impression. Despite its cavernous silence, there was a peacefulness, one I might even want to linger in if I could find a secluded space.

I was about to round a corner and enter into the nearest abode, when suddenly, a shuffling sound from inside made me reach for my sword, leaving it halfway sheathed until I knew the source.

"Who's there? Show yourself!" I said, surprised at my own gruff Arabic tone.

Stillness, then a rustling—and a slim shape holding a small oil lamp appeared in the doorway. A young woman wore a lose, transparent milky veil draped over her long dark hair, with a matching robe tightened at the waist by a crimson woven belt. She appeared younger than me, and despite the limited light that concealed her features, already I could make out their beauty. For a moment I stood speechless, perplexed at a vague sense of familiarity.

"What are you doing here?" I said, now adding some Greek to the Arabic. "It's not safe."

She made a sound almost like a muffled chuckle and slowly approached, but she was otherwise so quiet and fleet-footed that I initially thought I was dreaming or hallucinating. If it was a vision, Lord forgive me but it was the nicest one I'd seen since I'd left home.

She stood before me and motioned to the cross on my chest with a graceful wave, and pointed back at herself.

"You found us," she nodded, her glittering almond eyes overflowing with emotion that struck at my core. "You're a ghost-seer, because no one sees us," I thought she said with a tentative smile, her angelic voice leaving me awed and perplexed. It wasn't until later that I understood that she'd meant it exactly as she'd said.

Through our continued mutual efforts and hand gesturing, I gathered that her name was Maryam. She and her family were one of many Eastern Christians who'd been recently expelled from the Old City by governor Iftikhar al-Dawla. I had to suppress my mounting anger as I recalled that he'd been spared and escorted out of the city with his bodyguard. Since then, praying to avoid the chaos while hanging on to the hope of returning, she and her family had retreated to this area for safety, taking every care to avoid being seen and not lighting more lamps than necessary.

I told her we captured the city and were there to help the Christians, and her eyes glistened again at what I took to be the hopeful prospect of soon returning home. The thought of her seeing the bloodshed made my stomach lurch again, but knowing that some had been allowed to flee, along with the realization that she'd already seen her share of devastation offered little consolation.

I said I hoped to meet her again along with her family under better circumstances, and from her bashful smile I took it that she was in agreement. As parting gift she retrieved a bundle from her satchel and handed me a piece of flatbread, making me nearly salivate. At last after our ordeal, we would be eating well again, and I hoped that I'd share meals with her, too.

I left her and rejoined my kinsmen, pleading my God yet again that he would allow us to see each other again. And something in my heart pinched, because I knew then that if I was ever returning home, it wouldn't be without first ensuring she was safe.

The state of Jerusalem crowning our glory, along with those of Tripoli, Antioch, and Edessa, our fame was sealed into history. In celebration, we heeded Peter the Hermit's encouragement for all clerics, Greek and Latin alike, to make a thanksgiving procession to the Church of the Holy Sepulchre. Soon after, a council was held at the Holy Sepulchre to elect a king for the new Kingdom of Jerusalem. The wealthy, powerful Raymond of Toulouse and Godfrey of Bouillon, popular descendant of Charlemagne, were recognized as the leaders of the Crusade and the siege of Jerusalem, adding to their achievement as much as to their mounting mutual hostility. Godfrey was made Defender of the Holy Sepulchre, while Raymond refused all titles, and after being convinced by Godfrey to give up the Tower of David, he went on pilgrimage.

I had my own yearnings, and try as I might to steal away to see Maryam again, I implored for patience and humility in light of the lingering turbulent atmosphere. Any wavering zeal only revived when soon after, in Raymond's absence, the relic of the True Cross was found. A week later, we once more witnessed God's endless glory while led by Godfrey—the True Cross brandished in the vanguard—into victory at the coastal city of

Ascalon. We drove off the Fatimid army trying to take back our city, en-suring Jerusalem's security. But the sense of frailty never left, and it became more palpable each day when our troops returned home in droves—their vows fulfilled—leaving only three hundred knights and some two-thou-sand infantry to defend the land.

Aldric prowled like a restless lion as ever, so that I increasingly wished he'd leave as well. But with the changes in command he rose among the top ranks, and kept close his remaining followers, even if surely there had to be something in it for them. For my endurance and loyalty I was made knight by Robert of Flanders, with rights to my own chosen space in the Old City. While I'd expected nothing and still didn't know my future prospects, the thought of Maryam made me accept, even as I vowed to stay humble and not lord it over others, unless as necessary.

Yet this blessed change in my fortune didn't lessen my disgust at what was nothing less than Aldric's worsening displays of bestial ruthlessness, exceeding the natural urge to defend what we'd fought so hard for. Instead each day he became more and more the kind who descends further into evil from his presumed success, imagining himself an equal to God.

Thankfully, I passed increasingly more time away from the city, allowing me to learn more about the terrain, practice my Greek and Arabic, and most important of all, Maryam fast consumed all my thoughts. I told her about our plans to construct our fortress on Mons Gaudii to fend off the Saracens and shelter pilgrim convoys.

"I pray you will love and care for it as we do," said Maryam, and unrav-eled its long history, although I would've listened just for the pleasure of hearing her sweet, melodious voice. The mountain was revered as the burial place of prophet Samuel, along with his father Elkanah, and Saint Mary the Egyptian. Mar Samwil, its dedicated Greek monastery, had been built centuries before, and became a place of pilgrimage and hostel for Christian pilgrims on their way to Jerusalem. It had been restored and enlarged five centuries before in the reign of Emperor Justinian, who also claimed the surrounding defensive wall.

Once more, I was moved in ways that elated and unsettled me. There was so much to know and which I couldn't expect to not only find, but piece together on my own, try as I might. Because of Maryam, all the stories I'd imagined were now living and breathing in a different, visceral and palpable way. It was one thing to read them in the Bible and hear them at sermons, but to be there and walk in the footsteps of past pious men and women, rich and poor, from near and far—all yearning for and in service to Him, was both humbling and exalting. To know that we had power to protect these Christian holy sites, and witness its beneficial impact on local residents finally restored my purpose of being there after too long a pause. I wanted to help restore it all, not just for our glory, but for those who'd lived in the land and traced their roots back to the earliest Christian faithful.

"I've been patient and now I'd like to know what's been keeping you away," Aldric smirked one overcast day.

"Just getting to know the place. And since we've restored it to glorious Christian rule, we should welcome back those faithful who've been expelled," I said, doing my best to keep a light air, despite the mounting personal weight of the matter.

"Ah; at last, our man has found love," said Aldric, his light eyes boring into me.

"I don't know what you're talking about," I said, before I could even consider this urge to keep as much of that situation shrouded from him.

I'd meet Maryam in the afternoons and she eventually introduced me to her family of kind Greek Orthodox souls who doted on her and her younger brother. I was touched by their long family history that predated the arrival of the Saracens, their love for their land evident in their emotional recitals. They once possessed olive groves and though they had lost much of what had once been theirs, they could boast of family stories that took place in Jerusalem, and the since dilapidated Bethlehem and Ramallah.

"At least these can't be taken away," said Maryam. I saw a renewed purpose for my life, to help keep her stories alive and pass them on, and if she would have me, begin a new life with her. But even if she wouldn't—I couldn't ignore the realities of our different cultures that her parents might not approve of—I vowed to help her no matter how I could.

On a warm afternoon I confessed all this to her as one of our long walks took us up to the Mount of Olives. We passed by the area said to be Pelagia's humble dwelling—that reformed prostitute said to have lived in her cell as a man—and the Armenian church of Saint John the Baptist, the timeless air of religiosity enrobing us as if in a blessed dream. We strolled along, until we came to a stop at a hill with a breathtaking panoramic view overlooking the Old City and surrounding valley.

Standing there, absorbing the weight of the historic land that drank His blood could help soothe my own painful rejection, but to my eternal joy, she accepted my demand of her hand. Adding to my relieved surprise, she was confident that her parents would agree, and they had even hinted at such a union between us. All the doubts, all the darkness that had been part of this experience now receded with this development, and my heart sang at the realization that this had been my true crusade. All of it had been worth it, just for the chance to meet her and join my life with hers.

Like a forgiven sinner in heaven I floated on a cloud back to my quarters in the city, and informed Aldric that this step to resettle a family was now of urgency, as my own home was joyfully expanding.

"Ah, a local, then. I did say you could blend in," Aldric asserted, and for the first time I thought I read a hint of softness in his usually light, cold eyes.

Our date was set for fall, and I prepared my Old City quarters and an adjacent home for her parents, longing for her gentle, loving feminine touch to bless our new abode with her pure essence. For Maryam an overdue homecoming, for both of us a new beginning we longed for.

Daily I prayed at the nearby Holy Sepulchre, humbled tears burning my eyes at the thought that this blessed experience now included marrying her, right where our Savior had been crucified for us, his blood redeeming us like none other ever could. Already I imagined the stories she would tell me and our children, she who had breathed in the air and walked the Via Dolorosa long before I'd even thought of the possibility of going there myself.

We were not to see each other again until the day I went to get her on my locally bred stallion, but after a few days, I couldn't help it. At night I sneaked away to their dwelling, my heart pounding and filled with fear. I was so distraught that a shaking seized me and I had to stop to catch my breath. Hellish though the wait was, the wedding was just one more, final night away—I had to gather myself!

After a moment I went on despite my edginess, and thankfully I'd memorized the place so well that I could find it blindfolded. But the worst of all sounds seized me as I approached: dead silence.

I stopped, frozen in place.

Then a faint, electric buzzing. On and off, then louder, consistent like an accumulating gathering out of thin air.

My nostrils flared at the scent and I shook my head—denial filling me even as I began shaking uncontrollably. I lurched past the house, and there, to my horror, scattered fires revealed the worst sight I still have trouble shaking off—even after all this time.

Bodies—butchered everywhere; mutilated faces, disemboweled stomachs, scattered torn limbs. Carnage that made our taking of Jerusalem look mild in comparison, like a monster from the deepest pit of hell went through just for the pleasure of massacring every single person, creating as many pieces as possible. My bones rattled and I thought myself stuck, but for the violent, all-consuming urge propelling me to find her. She was *not* there, could *not* be there!

Needing to confirm my mounting, raging disbelief, I searched through the slaughtered bodies one by one, sickened by the constant sliced flesh even as I gave thanks that I saw no signs of her or her immediate family there. Escaped; they had escaped, I repeated to myself, trying to shake off my confusion at the sheer number of so many who hadn't. What was I then, but wild, faceless myself, somehow coherent enough to focus?

Then, I almost lost whatever consciousness I had left when I came upon her parents and brother. Bile caught in my throat, because while nearly unrecognizable, I could still make them out through their clothing and trinkets, and that faint, yet familiar knowing that forced angry tears out of me. The only thing that kept me from stopping right then, caught between needing to know and fearing to find the worst sight of all, was the absolute need to find her. Like a madman I searched, going under and over, repeatedly, and though I was no closer to knowing how or why this had happened, I knew for certain that she was not there.

I spent the night digging, assembling and burying the bodies, before hyenas, jackals, mountain lions, and anything else could come and claim more of this madness for themselves. Panting, I finally looked up to the hateful grey dawn sky, the heavenly day of our wedding transformed into a hellish nightmare.

Like a revengeful ghost I trudged back to my quarters, my drained soul feeding on its impending rampage for answers.

"Narduin! What in—" The refrain repeated several times until I realized it wasn't my imagination, but a younger follower of Aldric, approaching me along with others, all wearing variations of aghast expressions. I followed their roving eyes and only then realized the sticky crimson covering me, when none of this had even been my doing—the slain's blood still calling out for testimony beyond the grave.

"Where is—" The youngster stopped as I shook my head, and then everyone knew there would be no wedding.

"Cursed Saracens!" shouted Aldric, fast appearing from somewhere, his face contorting in yet a new way. "Who else could've done such a thing? They respect nothing, least of all a Christian's wedding day!"

Up to that moment I hadn't known what to think, but all I knew was that I would savor my hunting down of whoever was behind this evil carnage. I was already someone else: it was that instant.

My jaw clenched and heart raging, I wanted nothing more than to disappear, and hear and see nothing nor anyone. I vanished into my quarters, ransacking all the wine I could to numb my bursting pain. Where was she? Who had taken her? How would I ever find her now, in this world that had so fast become a living hell? How could I have thought that going there, to Jerusalem, would be any different! My throat burned as I drank, pacing back and forth like a lion in a cage as I tried to make some sense of this. I thought I heard the echo of ringing bells of a mass being said at the Holy Sepulchre, the tears forcing out what I tried but couldn't deny. Because I realized then that she could be dead, and all I could say was that I hadn't found her remains.

Racked with sobbing pain, I fell to my knees, the empty wine bottle crashing on the stone floor. An anguish, deeper than I'd ever experienced and that I wouldn't wish on anyone, seized me, the loss of her pure innocence calling forth my hate for all of humanity. Villains deserve their punishment; that sense of justice satisfies us, somehow. But that loss of innocence is always what breaks our hearts.

How had I failed her? While I was in heaven, preparing for our union, she and her family, who were to be mine, too, were suffering the worst of fates. That anyone would lay a finger on her—it called out something else in me that even I didn't like to see, that is more convenient to think I've long since mastered and has no power over me. Me: that so-called humble servant who swore I went on the mission seeking no reward. Amidst the deafening, piercing bells came a high-pitched cackle.

Doubling over in consuming pain, I saw myself at the bleeding feet of Jesus, nailed upon the cross, his flagellated flesh dripping holy blood down upon my tormented, unworthy face. How something could look so painfully vile yet immeasurably beautiful for its loving sacrifice is a mystery I'm not worthy of grasping—yet that I could be aware of that at the moment was a kind of humbling revelation in itself.

Ask and it shall be given, seek and you will find.

I heard it even amidst my shattering childlike sobs I was sure then would never end, like a warm cloak draped on me. My body rocked, and when I gazed upon the weight on my lap, there's not a place on this earth that my wailing didn't reach.

There lay Maryam, smaller than I remembered, looking like a sleeping angel in her white wedding robe and gold-embroidered veil I'd never had a chance to see her in—drenched in blood. Redness that left nearly no surface clean, yet her person, perfectly unblemished, so unlike the butchery of the scene. My love was such that, had she also been scattered in pieces, nothing would diminish her—anyone who saw her would know this, and some jealously despise her more for it. A cruel trick of the soul, selfish yet graceful: I would've gathered them and made her an eternal, glorious shrine, if only I could have a piece, something, anything remaining of hers!

I engulfed her in my arms, kissing her sleeping face, neck, hands, trying, respectfully, to see if she was wounded anywhere. But all that mattered then was that I hold her, treasure the little time I had with her before she disappeared again. I clung to her so tightly, our dark hair coiling that I almost thought she would awaken and look at me with her doe eyes, and say it was all a bad dream and we would never be apart. We were suspended for a moment, and I wanted nothing more than to remain there, together, forever.

I can bring her back, if only—sneered a familiar snake, tarnishing the vision, as it has done since the Garden of Eden.

When I awoke I was flat on the cold limestone floor, my wrathful anger ceding to gratitude to be alive, renewed with purpose. I had walked across nations to reach this city, and I would walk the whole earth until I found her.

I made my rounds, gathered everyone around, though I hardly needed to for their loyal understanding. Even with my own absence, I could already see things had changed further, a faithful yearning to serve in these men's eyes.

"So, will you be leaving too?" asked one.

"I wasn't planning on it, at least, not until I've resolved this," I said, feeling as cold as I sounded.

"With how occupied you've been, I just wanted to inform you: Aldric went missing for some days," said a second who'd been very faithful to him, confirming what I suspected.

"We know now, who he is. And we don't want to serve him anymore," said another.

"After everything he's given you?" I said.

"And taken, but no more. We know you and respect you, Narduin. You've always treated us well, never used us or pitted us against each other. We'd like to prove ourselves to you, if you'll allow us. However we can, we are at your service," said the first.

"Seems we all have to be careful, thinking we know someone. That can always change," I sneered. Despite my own unusual tone, I read the honesty in their eyes, so racked themselves that I thought I'd cry anew, in a different way. None of us were as innocent as we wished anymore, and once more, I would challenge my own self-control.

"Tonight. Gather, stay close, and at my signal," I said, their demeanors brightening with new light.

The evening couldn't come fast enough and at last, we gathered for the usual drinking and feasting, the ancient thick stone walls closing in around us merging with my new and older supporters. I knew better than to show my own tormented soul, and I wasn't even sure what I was feeling anymore. I drank freely, my blood boiling under my usual cool exterior.

"Good Narduin. I'm surprised yet gratified to see you in better enough spirits to join us. From what I know of you, I thought it would take longer," said Aldric, studying me.

"I thought so, too, and I felt lost at first. But being here has changed us, reminded us of what's really important," I said, the weight of eyes on me at every corner.

"Very true," he said, impressed despite his sly attempt to dig into me.

"I realize I've been selfish, and I will release it. All for the better," I said, and caught two pairs of eyes in the crowd as I looked around, then looked back to his frowned expression.

"Surely. But you love her; it's normal to be angry," said Aldric, his feigned surprise bordering on annoyance.

"In a way. But what will anger do? Bring her back? Like anyone can do this? No, only Jesus can." I fixed him hard. "Only Jesus can!" I yelled with a voice I hardly recognized, and everyone swarmed on him, hauled him down the stairs to a concealed secret basement, and tied him up to a chair so fast that I didn't need to do a thing, had I wanted to. They were enjoying themselves, and almost gagged him until I nodded to leave the cloth hanging around his neck.

"Narduin, what is this? What have they put you up to?" Aldric panted.

"Oh, Aldric. You know. You see, no Saracen could've known of our wedding, and if they did, it was from you."

I was already a private person by nature, and from the beginning I'd wanted no one's opinions; no opportunity for separation between she and I, kept like a concealed treasure until finally she was officially my wife. My wrath coiled up slowly, sensing he was all too aware of this.

"What? What are you saying? You think that I would do this to you? Why would I?" He stared, searching. "What did they tell you? Whatever's happened with them, it's got nothing to do with us; you know this!" I'd never seen his eyes dart that way, his pitiful look that made him resemble a helpless boy. And though I believed none of it, it only fueled my hate more to see how convincing he could make it.

"I know you're capable of many things, Aldric. We all are," I said, and he shrank in the echo of resounding sneers united as one.

"Narduin, please, this is a mistake. Please, release me!"

"Perhaps." I smiled, approaching him. "As soon as I get the information I need." His jaw tightened at the sight of my prompt blade. Such vanity. I swore I could hear his childish thoughts, worried I'd scar his spoiled nobleman's face—and it made me want to even more.

"What—are you going to do?" Aldric mumbled so piteously it's a miracle I didn't end him right then and there.

"Where's the fun in telling you? Plus I think you already know. You've always given me the impression that you knew more than you let on." I grinned, tracing the knife's edge down his cheek, neck, chest. It glided all the way down to his lower torso, crossing side to side. Everyone else smiled then, except him, and though I wanted to fully match theirs, I was just too empty.

"Please, Narduin, please, I beg you. Don't hurt me." His tone became husky then, until I fixed him a hard gaze and he diminished, realizing at last we had different ends. Where he would amplify and terrorize, I would castrate and banish. It wasn't just the first horrible, sickening memory of self-banishment creeping over him contorting his face, but the realization that I could be even stronger than him, who'd thought himself invincible.

"That's possible. Just tell me where she is."

"I don't know! I swear, I don't!"

I sighed. "As you wish. I will have my answer either way, that is a promise. I'll revisit you each day and ask you the same. That should give you time enough to dig deep and think."

"Think? There's nothing to think about because I don't know! Please, Narduin! How can you do this to your superior? After everything we've achieved!"

"As you see," I shrugged, proud at myself for hiding the disgust he inspired.

"No, please! Don't leave me here! I'll suffocate!"

I retreated with the men and told them I'd personally check on him, assuring that I'd enlist their help as soon as it was needed. Despite their limited involvement, I sensed their instant relief at his contained presence, although I didn't share that feeling. Maybe they put too much trust in me—an endearing credulity—or maybe my hate surpassed even theirs to allow to be so soon relieved, maybe both.

As promised, each day I returned alone, and I had to suffer through his repeated pleas of innocence. I had the sense of waiting for that answer, although I had no idea how it would come, and least of all that it would come from him. Time stood still, each moment like barren days until I'd face him again, and I'd be left as empty as before.

"Please, I beg you. Just a sip. It's been two days already!" Aldric screamed as he saw me approaching, like he'd saved his breath just to say this. "I know you, you don't mean this! I'd tell you if I knew!"

Pitiful, meaningless words were all that came out of him.

"Two days? Is that all?" Clouds of heat clung to the air as I paced around him, making sure the bonds held tight, and I had a mind to drape layers of chains on him, too. But one must hold back, tease and pace one's torture; that's the pleasure of it.

"Please, I'll do anything, *anything* else that I can!"

"Until tomorrow," I said, deaf to his cries, and gladly left him panting, whatever patience I had left fast wearing thin.

The next day I found his head drooping to the side, and it took a moment before I could revive him.

"Just as I thought: progress!" I yelled, and slapped him a few times. "Now, for the last time, where is she?"

Aldric looked up at me like his life was over, when we both knew it was only beginning. One life, into the next—that's all it ever was and would ever be, into eternity.

"I—don't—know." His lips drooped and eyes pinched shut, and then, most amazingly: tears, hovering, hating to admit defeat. "Do I have to die too, for you to believe me?"

"Oh, Aldric. Even now, in this pitiful state, you're still flattering yourself. No one's life means a thing to me now," I said, the words horrifying me with their potential repulsive truth.

That's when I knew: it would never really stop, I'd never be at peace until I had my answers. A cry thundered in my soul: and what if I was wrong? And I was wrong, would continue to be wrong—until I found her. There *was* the answer; I just had to find it, no matter how. That's all I had to go on, and I would not back down.

My knife was in his face before I consciously knew it, and a million unleashed demons swarmed, telling me what to do: pierce here, there, anywhere at all, so long as I began somewhere—the rest would follow, like all the repeated chaos I'd been a part of.

You're not innocent, you deserve this!

The accusations resounded, and maybe I did—but *she* didn't! That even then, after everything, I, being who I was, that beast among beasts, knew this had to prove that I wasn't completely beyond redemption. So I did what I always do: I silenced them. I was the one in charge, not them. Suddenly, I recalled Jesus and the swine and a stillness overcame me.

"Time has come, Aldric. It's the blessed third day," I smirked.

"I—need," he drooled, his grotesque drooping eyes annoying me more by the second.

"Yes, you do need. By the blood of Jesus, tell me your name," I said, brandishing my crucifix from under my robe and hovering it over his face. His head flew up, his piercing blank eyes staring in a new, and yet familiar way. "By the blood of Jesus, tell me your name!" I yelled.

A deep, vicious groan echoed, and slowly, his jaw widened like a roaring demon. Unearthly sounds blasted out—unclean, deafening shrieking.

"By the blood of Jesus, you *will* tell me your name!" I screamed, and stepped up to bury the cross hard on his forehead. A whirl of energy engulfed me and though I could hardly understand how I got there, to this moment, the power was both humbling and addicting. Aldric gasped in his vibrating chair, his rasped breathing shaking him so that I almost thought he might break out of his bonds. I had seen a lot by then, but this was different still, as it always is—another test to face. His breath stilled, his face once more shifting from the way I knew it. Grinning, his head tilted back and let out a mocking cackle. "Awar and Dasim, sons of Iblis."

Somehow I managed not to laugh. Tales from around the fire—these demon sons of Iblis: Awar who encourages debauchery and Dasim, causer of enmity between man and wife—resurfacing here. Even if fitting to be his demons, it was almost too predictable.

"And what else, Aldric?" I said, stepping back as I held tight to the cross, the rightful barrier maintained between us.

His head turned to the side, one eye looking at me unnaturally, painfully, from its corner. Another cackle, inhuman, exaggerated.

"More, there's more! There are many of us, who've been here from long ago!" His face nearly whiplashed back to face me again, though if the blackness of his eyes were real or imaginary, I couldn't say. "And you can't hide from us; we see you! Do you know how long he, we, all of us, wanted to do this! To really unleash all our rightful justice, establish our order? You do, because your legion is there, too, just waiting for you! Those Jews and Saracens, Saracens and Jews, over and over and over—and what about *you*! You're their servants you know; they never tire of reminding you, and the whole world of it. But together, we are more; *we* did this! We made it happen, even you! And now the kingdom is ours! But the work must be done from beginning to end! No loose ends, and your little love was distracting you. Yes, you know it! You should've seen how glorious it was, how I searched and slithered my way, eating corpse after corpse, yearning for hers most—you know it all too well, you can't deny me this. Yes, and I had to stop you from mixing with those inferiors. You who had resisted so long, one sight of a local peasant girl and you're gone? Such weakness!"

I lunged at him and wrapped my hands around his throat.

"Weakness? You're right, you'd know weakness, because that's what *you* are. But in Him, oh, I can do all things! You should know this best of all!" I squeezed but even amidst his gurgling mouth, his twisted, reddened face shook in grotesque laughter.

"It's too late! If I can't find her, then neither will you!" Aldric yelped.

A divine madness seized me, because somehow I heard the truth in his lies. My vision blurred, clouded by hot tears, and I had to pull myself off of him before I squeezed whatever breath he had left out of him. I wanted to do any and every painfully horrible thing to this disgusting mass of life, as if it could satisfy—but what would it change? I would not give him the satisfaction and I wished nothing more than to never see him again. I backed away and he quieted down, blinked, and from his tired demeanor I knew he was back, whatever difference that really made. I knew then that I didn't care, if this was all a showy display of the strength of his twisted soul, or genuine possession, or some other odd combination, because I had one answer. He had not, and would not get to her.

I flew to my own quarters, pacing, trying to pray, anything to get me focused, but all I could do was drift back south to the site of her and her family's last moments. It was as desolate as before, but the eternal rumble of echoes consumed me, and through my sobs I repeated prayers to the family, begging for something that would tell me of her fate. Aldric was the epitome of self-satisfying lies, but the worst was that he was right and I might never and didn't deserve to know, and now had to humble myself to this state of being, until and if He ever decided to change it.

What had I known of Maryam, except for our brief moments of joy, as perfect as they were? Had I been so blind in my love? She could've left, maybe even lied about her feelings for me. Had I pressured her somehow; had she been afraid of me, thinking she had to agree so that I, one of the wild crusaders, wouldn't hurt her and her loved ones? The fullness of what we represented hit me only then like sacks of stones, at how selfish I could've been not to give this more attention. All I hoped for then was that she lived, and was safe and happy no matter where she was, and I feared that my erratic prayers weren't strong enough for her to know that.

I told the men of my closed case with Aldric, advising they do the same. Even with what I shared, we could come to no other conclusion that he was indeed possessed, though of what only God knows. The gazes mixed with fear and hate, somehow tamed with satisfaction at the unfolding and the promise of instilling their own justice, reminded me they'd known of this in their own cruel way. If nothing else, there was the shared sense that we were doing the world a favor. And if Aldric was as powerful and knowledgeable as he feigned, then let him find a way out of it, as he had before, surely to his advantage.

But knowing his real name, and that I was allowed to serve Jesus, as flawed as I was, we both knew that he had no real power over me. Best of all, it was our kept secret, and if anyone asked about his whereabouts, we settled on saying we'd last seen him that feasting night. After all, he was well-known for visiting the underground taverns, and he'd often been advised by others to steer clear of the worst ones, which naturally, were also his favorites.

Craving escape, I shed my crusader garb for simple linen robes, my dark shaggy beard and hair still a much better sight than my drained spirit. I retreated to the Mount of Olives, where I paced for hours around the place where she'd agreed to be mine. Try then as I could to be objective in reviewing my memories, I couldn't see a trace of dishonesty in her, and I resolved that even if she had indeed misled me, then my love was too strong to hold it against her. Days elapsed, one like the next, as I drifted along the ancient caves of ascetics, and the cloister for women followed by another for men built by Melania the Younger.

There I wallowed, with believers of all kinds—Roman, Greek, Armenian, Arab—dwelling silently there, and amidst my emptiness I found a quiet repose. Though my sadness would never leave and had become a part of me, it was less painful there, in the stillness and simplicity that I was sure she'd practiced herself. I tried to take comfort in imagining that she'd approve of my choice of being there.

Dreams, visions, nightmares, hallucinations—for they blurred into one—tormented me. *Wait on the Lord, wait on the Lord,* and it occurred to me that maybe it was my calling to join them instead, and had been all along. It wasn't betrayal, if that was where I belonged, and even if it didn't look like what my brethren, or even I, had imagined, it didn't mean I couldn't still serve our Lord we'd all come this long way for. I'd been so confused about where to be in this land, and after being with Maryam, this was the only place that made sense and helped me forget myself as I walked in His holy steps.

The last time I saw the men, they blessed my choice, surprised that I'd even ask after the high rank I'd acquired for myself. Nothing would change that, and they promised to visit often, all wearing smiles I'd never seen before. One chapter was also done for them, and that they had found some sense of peace after the chaos gladdened my heart, too.

If it was heresy to leave my parents' Catholic church for another, then I am guilty of it, as I've been of many other things. But He looks at the heart and knows I didn't betray Him there; rather I joined it with her church, elevating our brief love to something unfathomably, and perfectly spiritual. Though I wouldn't utter it that He could not be contained to one church—I had seen too much to think differently—it didn't change the truth, and I longed to dwell with her memory in that way, and be One in Christ as Galatians 3:28 says.

The day of my profession of vows came, and I was as nervous as on our impending wedding—that best and worst day of all, where your vulnerability and strength are exposed and tested for all to see. For a time I kept my eyes averted, though I was ultimately thankful that it would be seen. What was I doing there? Maybe it was time to go home once and for all.

The priest called my name in his Eastern accent I'd grown to love, for it reminded me of hers. It enveloped me once more, lovingly reprimanding, and then, I knew I'd drifted off again in my miraculous wish, because it wasn't him anymore, but another voice—the one I truly wanted to hear.

"Hanna? Hanna Shayb! Narduin of Flanders! How's that herring coming along?"

I resurface back into that Christian Palestinian man I am, basking in her glorious voice calling me out of my reverie, beaming as I come to. Not unlike I did then.

"I thought that's who you were thinking of," says Nawal. "But you can leave him there sometimes, too. I like us as we are, now."

"Me, too."

And as she wraps her arms around me, as we did when we fell into each other over nine hundred years ago when I thought I'd lost her, my heart bursts that we keep finding each other through the chaos. It will always be this achingly beautiful way: Christian Middle Eastern souls spread out and calling to each other across the world. It's been so long and though we've changed, some memories linger more powerfully than others, no matter how impossible and unexplainable they seem.

Even if I wanted to, I can't recreate every memory down to the last detail. That hardly happens in one life, let alone multiple ones. But since I don't want to fully separate myself from what happened then, I treasure what's remained: that humbling proof that our vow was as real then as it is now, and will only keep growing.

Whatever doubts I had of my sanity were soon washed away, learning that she'd also sneaked out to see me the night before the wedding. Alerted by noise, it was then that she'd seen who marched upon them, and horrified to lose both her family and me, had fled to safety at the holy, sanctified Mount of Olives. Without a word she handed her pained prayers to Him, remembering nothing good and of worth was her, or my, doing. Her perfect, trusting patience, that nothing can overcome, kept us both safe until the moment of our rightful reunion. Then and now, we are one soul, and it was more, and always will be, more than I could've asked for.

I thought I would find utter peace, and only peace, in Jerusalem, and I did, all because of her. We went to Jerusalem, but the truth is that we also went to the darkest pits of hell. And though light and dark are mercifully separate, I learned to what unrelenting extent the darkness lurks close, clinging, seeking its entrance, and what constant hard work it is to keep it at bay.

I'm grateful for the enduring power of this memory, when our God-made-flesh suffered the cruelest death there, and so many have marched upon it, eager to call it their own. How often I've lamented that each time in history when we had a chance to gather and grow closer as One eternal Christian community, we strayed, letting other things get in the way of this eternally sacred mission. But with Him, all things are possible, and I dare to know that one holy blessed day it will be so.

With each lesson, some things will and won't change, and as I keep learning, it's not lost on me that these days nearly anyone can be proud of who or what they are, in spite of—and sometimes especially for—warts and all, except a Christian, because then that's just too problematic. As if there aren't variations there, too, or other religions are blameless, or more importantly, like anything—including our constant petty squabbling—could ever diminish His greatness.

How easily we forget that He's the only One who can and should be shared and leaves no one wanting—the One who cannot be drained by our insatiable, incessant longing, even as that urge is the remnant of our yearning to return to Him, whether we're conscious of it or not.

A servant of Jesus will always be a crusader, and graced with the light that shines in darkness, the next time it will be better.

THE ROBBER BRIDEGROOM'S WIFE

SOMEWHERE IN THE BLACK FOREST

There's a feeling like a kind of peace as we stand there, she and I, watching his body swing gently, side to side, hypnotizing us as we stare. Contained and exposed for all to see, at last put to rest by the tightening rope. Could it be that it's really over? For so long my life had been so structured, prey to his incurable sickness; he the invincible ruler of his domain that I once thought would never end. Strange thing it is, that when it changes you just might wonder at the unexpected void present—unsure what to fill it with.

I see her: the other young maiden he'd planned to marry—unaware of her peculiar resemblance to me—a faint grin forming at the corner of her lips, proud of herself for the desired turn of events. And as I feel a soft, warm wind blow, I smile at her youthful glow, porcelain skin, and light green eyes, and I marvel that I ever was—or is it still am?—that young. And yet I wonder: can I go back to how I was before? I've worn this face for so long that I could almost forget that I've ever had another. How long does it take to turn back the clock: the answer that has yet to come.

He will never know that it was his smile that caught me. The perfect, evenly-shaped white teeth behind full sensuous lips, towered by two ebony glistening eyes and bushy raven eyebrows. The allure of the obscurity diffused through his gaze, coupled with his gleaming grin, and I knew that he'd be mine. My life once so tranquil amidst our beautiful countryside, simple, perhaps uneventful to unsuspecting eyes. But I liked that feeling of having a secret; my sense of sometimes knowing things others didn't.

Our cottage on a farm outside the forest, plain suitors coming in day by day. My answer always the same: *No, no, no: I feel absolutely nothing*. The concerned drooping of my father's head, wanting his precious gifted daughter to be well taken care of—quickly before her time was up. He knew, in a way, but could never fully grasp it; this *magic aura* about me, as he called it. I'd spend all day in the woods: heard and saw things not everyone did, wasn't afraid the way others were; too drawn to that other ethereal realm. I knew how things could be deceiving, that what seemed frightening often wasn't once you approached it. He taught me well, as much as he could as a lone parent. And though most would say my mother was gone, to me it was more like she'd just changed forms. And so, though he meant well, I couldn't understand his distress—so sure was I that I already had all I ever wanted.

And then *he* appeared, from a place I'll never really know, knocking right at our door as if he knew exactly that it was me he was coming for. Fruitful dinner conversations and father growing hopeful at his—and my—lack of reservation, thankful at the concept of this chance meeting with such an accomplished prospect. I blushed, looking away as my suitor's eyes bore through me across the table—the growing strange feeling in the pit of my stomach that I both loved and doubted. Who was this man to have this effect on me? The flash of lightning that was his smile striking me straight in the heart, and it was no longer mine; my mysterious admirer shattering my world and making me long for something I didn't know existed.

It grew: this hunger that I'd never had before, to be united with someone who might understand, accept things about you others wouldn't. A sense of salvation like I'd finally found my match—someone with whom to share a secret, knowing it wouldn't be betrayed.

Why did you accept?

You make me feel different, I said. He drew me nearer and his piercing gaze reached so deep I thought my very life would always depend on him looking at me that way.

We were the happiest creatures on earth that idyllic summer of our blooming love, filling us with endless longing for our future that seemed boundless. As in a dream I stepped into his—now our—beautiful large castle, whose high ceilings and marble staircases adorned with tasteful furniture and colorful tapestries each took my breath away. Was it real?

Awed as I was by all of it, I secretly craved the fulfilment of that union that made so many maidens blush and giggle. I'd imagined it before, the way I'd feel at that moment, but nothing ever compares to the actual event. Strong, gentle, commanding, yielding—everything I'd envisioned and more. Cautious, too soft even—and somehow I almost swore he wasn't being himself. He *didn't want to scare me,* he said, but something overcame me and I wondered how he could ever think such a thing, and it wasn't long before we both got exactly what we wanted.

Time had stopped, it seemed. He was always there, giving me what I wanted in every way—absorbed, lost in our world of all-consuming passion—discovering, and then, natural, familiar to each other's flesh. He and I: there was nothing else. I was his and I liked it; wasn't that how it was supposed to be? My other half, my husband who would ensure my happiness and fulfill my dreams, and I for him. I felt utterly exposed, and a few times I even thought I'd do it then: reveal that other aspect of myself concealed within. What would he think? I'd never shared it and I wasn't sure I was ready to do it. With everything so perfect, it was so easy to forget myself and leave it as was, to be brought up some other time.

I noticed him a few times clutching his head, a look of deep agony—or was it rage?—in his eyes. But he said it was nothing, just a headache that my embraces would instantly help dissipate.

The fire grew, fulfilling, and then, also sometimes frightening me. His strong, eager hands gripping my body, fingernails burying deep in my flesh, I felt his hard bite; his teeth drawing blood on my neck leaving bruises that remained for days. The coldness of a sharp silver blade upon my warm, dewy skin—tracing up and down my body, sometimes tearing through corset and fabric. Infernal: his frowning eyes as if possessed when holding me, a prisoner in his arms, so different from his quiet charm. My wifely privilege: seeing a hidden part of him that only came out during such private moments.

Bold, but not too bold!—and though I didn't know the reason, the phrase echoed from somewhere deep within my soul.

You're going to kill me, he said as I lay in his arms in bed one night. *But I can't lose you*, he added, his kiss closing in on me before I could protest. How could I ever be the same after him? Loving him changed everything.

Eventually he announced our marriage to his colleagues, so we prepared a feast to host them. They were educated handsome young men, but try as I might I couldn't shake the unpleasant feeling I had from them. Pompous and boisterous, they seemed so different from him, but I assumed it was a different matter when it came to their work relations. Soon after, he announced he was leaving with them to attend to business a few towns away, thus leaving me alone in our large beautiful home for the first time.

I realized I hadn't been out much at all since my arrival, and I took the chance to explore the house and gardens of my new abode. The rooms were striking: large, well-furnished with intricate wood pieces, damask velvet and satin fabrics, bronze Roman statues, and porcelain decorations. But all the same, the rooms were all imbued with an air of loneliness. Surely this place was quite spacious for a man without a family, something that would likely soon change.

One sunny day I proceeded out, starting with the back gardens. I instantly noted the tall discolored grass and identical stone fountains on each side covered in growing vines. Tall, thick shrubs lined the perimeter; a kind of fence marking the confines of the grounds. The neglected state made it clear no one had spent time there recently. Turning around, I went along the side of the towering castle to access the front gardens, and a quick glance up to the dark walls suddenly made me shudder. It never seems to make sense when it happens, but something about the shade cast a gloomy, almost threatening air on the property.

To my surprise the front gardens had even taller grass, almost reaching my waist, so that the only walkable area was the center pebble-strewn path that crunched under each step. Once more, overgrown bushes encircled the domain, ensnaring the massive ornamental metal spiked fence. Further beyond still was the dense forest, the foliage rendered nearly pitch black in the distance. I smirked, because although newly married, somehow I knew that it was quite like him. If it was peace, quiet, and privacy he'd wanted—and I suspected he did—this place surely offered it. I made a note to tease him about the gardens' conditions upon his return: what a contrast from the well-kept interior.

At last a commotion announced his return, and I rushed to him in happy longing. And yet he felt different, hardened—but not like before where it would instantly yield to his concealed softness beneath the surface. The coldness in his manner shocked me—I'd never seen him that way before—but I pretended not to notice and promptly set up his dinner, for surely he was famished after such a long journey. We ate silently, mostly, for he gorged down the steaks I made as if he hadn't eaten in weeks, while casting sharp glances at me. I pinched a smile, eager to suppress the odd heavy feeling sweeping over me.

Once finished, I started clearing the table when he suddenly swiftly maneuvered behind me, his arms engulfing me as he kissed; first my ears, cheek, and jawline, until I felt his strong hand close around my neck, forcing me to look at him. His manner was rougher than it'd ever been, almost as if wanting to go against my will—and I realized I wasn't sure if he was just teasing. We locked eyes. *This dinner isn't always going to suffice*, he said, and though part of me wanted to dismiss it with a chuckle, I was too caught off guard to do anything but silently comply.

I awoke the next day alone in bed. My head was pounding, and it took me some time to come to my senses. Mustering my strength, I reached for the water basin on the nearby dresser, splashed cold water on my face, and I realized I could hardly remember what had happened. The last thing I recalled from the previous night was kissing, drinking wine, more loving... and that was it. I was drained, sore, and though part of me wanted to linger in bed, I forced myself up, hoping that motion would rouse me out of the strange stupor.

I slipped out of my night robe to change into my brocade gown, and I almost screamed: my body was covered in red-pink marks all over. My eyes roamed frantically, my fingers reluctantly grazing all over my skin. For an instant I thought maybe I'd contracted some illness, but some probing elicited pain from the tender bruises. I noted some had traces of small rectangular shapes, and though I tried to dismiss it, I knew all too well what they were: teeth marks. My body remembered what I didn't: an outline tracing the path, the assaulted skin surface moments away from breaking. And yet he'd stopped—why? And then, what I dreaded asking: would he next time?

Once dressed I went downstairs, and found his note stating he'd return later that evening. All day I tried to make sense of it: was that his idea of rough play? But why wouldn't he tell me about it? *He didn't want to scare me,* I heard the echo of his words in my thoughts, but I couldn't help but feel that wasn't it. Putting my knowledge to use, I applied some herbal potions to my skin, and by the afternoon the fading bruises were already starting to heal. I tried to keep busy doing my usual daily activities—reading, tidying, cooking—my thoughts always trailing back to our love. Could it be some misunderstanding?

When he returned I teased him about the marks and he grinned, tilting his head as he stared, gentle as ever, saying it was my fault for making him get carried away. He kissed and massaged the bruises, seemingly pleased at my playful acquiescence. And though part of me wanted to dismiss it as some minor event, I sensed something was changing.

His absences became more common, and I noticed his edgy, altering temper, so much that I started wondering if something was wrong, perhaps with work or his companions. Were things going badly? He did seem to be quite uneasy when returning from their outings. But I tried not to probe into his private matters; not wanting to remind him of trouble when he was home and away from the potential source of it all.

Sometimes he didn't come home at all, and my nights were filled with disrupted sleep marred by disturbing images. Cackling, shouting voices shrouded in thick smoke, gold coins, and the sickening scent of alcohol. Louder, louder, the deafening mocking laughter, almost drowning out the echoes of a woman's screams, stifled—a scuffle? Blood everywhere. Then, always, it stopped, overcome by some shadow I couldn't see. Other nights I dreamt of him sitting there, at the edge of our bed, his entire shape pitch black like some demon, staring at me with his bright scarlet eyes and bloody gaping mouth—waiting. I'd awake, panting and covered in sweat, calling out to him to see if he was there—finally back from who knows where—and though he wasn't, it was as if the place was haunted.

One day I went down to the cellar—that part of the castle I rarely visited—intent on choosing some Riesling to go with my prospected chicken dinner. Clutching my candelabra I made my way in the long, dark chilly stone room, and I would've been out quickly from the eerie place, as I planned, but some strange impulse compelled me to proceed further down to the far back. It struck me to find tables covered in empty bottles, as if there'd been a lively gathering there at some point. Why in such a cavernous place and why hadn't it been cleaned up? But surely it had simply been missed in such an immense castle, so I turned to leave until a glint caught my eye. I crept to a corner lined with large wine barrels, my searching eyes finding little bright pearls on the floor. For a moment I simply stared, confused. I knelt down and picked them up, confirming it was a woman's necklace—filling me with overpowering dread. Nearly losing my balance I grabbed onto one of the barrels, the pull inadvertently bringing it closer to me. I made to push it back in place when I saw a bright fabric and pulled it out to inspect it: a woman's crimson satin gown, slashed and covered in dark stains. I traced the rips in the dress as if I knew what had happened, because I realized then and there that I did. My body tensed as I held the final proof of his true self. How could I keep dismissing what there was no more denying? And so I vowed that I would protect myself, and in any way possible maintain the upper hand, for he wouldn't know my secret until I revealed it.

That night I waited until he finished—chewing hungrily as he always did. And it was harder than I thought it'd be, to behold his handsome face and have to reveal that I knew his secret, concealed wickedness.

You have something to tell me, I said, and this time it was I who bore intently into his soul. I tried, wanting to make myself strong, doing all I could to keep the tears from clouding my vision, and though they were held back I know he saw them. I read confusion in his face, wrestling with so many conflicting emotions: defeat, anger, betrayal, hatred. To think that part of him might have felt revulsion towards me hurt most, but I couldn't deny that I'd seen it. Finally he seemed to take on a cold distant air, and I noted his hands turning to fists as he got up to come towards me.

Don't, I said, and he knew that I wouldn't let him near me.

What are you saying? he asked, his tone almost pleading. *You don't—No. You don't understand, it's just something I need once in a while*, he said.

You're not the same, it's changing, I said, watching his every move.

Curses! Don't you see me trying! he yelled, pounding the redwood table with his massive fists.

Keeping my distance, we continued our even pacing around the table, and I saw through his concealed calculations to outdo me. After a moment his palms covered his face, the fingers gradually scraping down, burying into his eye sockets—groaning as his breathing slowed.

I'm not gonna hurt you—I haven't hurt you, he said after a pause, seemingly calmer now.

But you did. You drugged me, I finally said it, for how else could I have forgotten that night and those bruises?

He seemed shocked, although if it was due to my knowledge or that I would accuse him, I couldn't say.

But you weren't hurt! he snapped, seemingly confused at the accusation. And he became so distressed, rubbing his temples as he groaned, that for a moment I thought he would start to cry. *Oh, oh it's so hard!* he moaned. *But I didn't hurt you! No! I held back!* He cast me the most innocent glance. *You don't know—No; you don't know how you help me. With you around it's already gone down, if only you knew...*

And for a moment I believed him—I really wanted to. And though I longed to run to comfort him, I stayed in place as he retreated, vanishing somewhere in the vast castle.

That night I cried, knowing things would never be the same, starting with keeping to our separate rooms—now aware I'd have to constantly be on my guard. For though I'd tried I could no longer lie to myself: his darkness was deeper than mine had ever been, or would ever be. In fact it was of a different nature entirely. But I tried, oh I tried to excuse it: after all, what had I really seen? Did I truly know what I was dealing with? Perhaps I was misunderstanding; for what did I really know of myself, of him, of love and all these tormenting feelings? Maybe I was inventing things that weren't really there; new experiences clouding my mind, trying to scare me. But why would I—when I was so eager to find him blameless for everything—and I usually did. But how much can you ignore before reaching your limit?

I fended off his darkness for a short time, but I knew deep down it wouldn't last. Always the hope though; that's what you do when you're in love. Hope, no matter how much the facts show you otherwise. Still, I tried hard to make myself trusting, reminding myself of my own power as my secret leverage. Did I really have to be afraid? But then I was constantly reminded that he wasn't just this one person, this handsome successful man I loved: he was also someone else, a despicable monster that I had to keep at bay.

He tried: fighting it with all his might—gorging his food with such ferocious appetite; anything to take his mind away from the fact that it wasn't me he was tasting. Each night, I prepared and served him a different meal, lying to myself that it would be enough; that perhaps he just needed to try another kind of animal meat—and our lives could somehow reach a semblance of normalcy. But I knew it was only a matter of time before he'd finally come for me.

Broad shoulders raised, chest heaving, panting wildly, curved claws breaking furniture, his angry bloodshot eyes glued on me, and my time was up: I could not escape. So at last I surrendered—not to him, but to myself—channeling my inner concealed powers as he watched, frozen in place. I hadn't wanted it this way, to have to reveal it in such circumstance. How different things could've been, maybe I could've even taught him things... but it was not to be. I'd not let him have me, not in that way.

I felt it all with the pain of a thousand knives: my strength diminishing, skin discoloring, thinning, sagging away from my bones; my blond hair overcome by greyness, my lips drying and face wrinkling—the kind he'd never want or long for, and I would be safe. Safe, and cursed to remain for I could not escape; my love of the little good in him too strong to give up on it. And I knew as it happened that I'd stay and watch over him, as a look of shocked distaste remained on his face—one outcome that stopped him from his unnatural intent. Amidst the ordeal that was our lives, at least I could be there, try to help somehow; maintain some order out of chaos. Not that I had much choice: my world turned upside down, nowhere to go and no one to turn to, the final proof revealed that the man I love is a brutal beast ready to devour me, as he'd done so many others. Stunned and overcome, perplexed at the revelation of my power, his dawning fear that I could escape his grip ceded to the knowledge that he couldn't do a thing about it. Torn between wanting me gone and always there: our fates connected by our secrets.

My days became like cyclic tormenting nightmares; perpetually hounded by his unruly emotions, topped by his insulting sneers that I'd become this ugly old crone no one would care about.

Revolting, decrepit, without purpose.

And I'd cry myself to sleep, consoled by the thought that he surely said it to spite me rather than out of sincerity. His attention gone, left alone in the large abode in the woods, my tears would mix with the soapy water on the floor, as I tried in vain to scrub away the piercing pain of his cruelty that struck at my core. Yet, there were occasional days when I'd catch my breath, sensing him staring at me, the way he did when I'd looked young and beautiful. Silent as a ghost, standing in the shadows, attentively watching.

Nothing has changed, he'd repeat, clawing his head in his hands—*You're still the same.* And I knew that he'd never harm me, suspicious yet comforted he was by the knowledge that he was loved despite his dark ways.

The veil of illusion and etiquette dropped, blurring the line between anguish and nonchalance as the constant stream of bodies came piling in—radiant, beautiful girls—drugged up to be devoured as he and his psychotic friends wished. I pitied their fates, so different from the way it'd been between us. Their rosy flesh he'd relish; tearing through raw tough meat, thick blood smearing his face, his reddened skin rejuvenated after each chunk he had. Servant to his curse: his greed fathomless, the ephemeral nature of his satisfaction.

Like clockwork I'd watch him transform into that drunken monster, ripping off clothes and biting into fresh limbs, as their screams went unheard in the castle, smothered by the clustered trees in the dark of night. I knew of things like potions that could help—lessen the pain, render them unconscious—and I'd slip it to the girls, who'd become dazed and numb to his ravenous desire. But I had to temper it—not too strong a dose or it'd knock them out instantly—lest he'd discover my trick, but he was usually too wild in the moment to even notice. I felt powerless at the sight of such abomination, knowing it was him, and yet, not; the tentative excuses doing nothing to lessen the horror of what I witnessed. Even when he had his moments of calm, it made no difference; later redoubling his efforts to such an extent that it canceled it all out, almost as if making up for lost time. At times I wondered if I could make him change—perhaps summon some ancient knowledge unlike anything I'd ever tested. And though deep down

I thought I could, I dared not think what it meant of me that I wasn't sure I wanted to risk myself for the mere possibility of saving him.

Year after year, it went on, his charisma faithfully seducing countless women, his captivating smile spreading wide at the thought of the constant feasting. And I wondered about them: who they were, what their lives were like, but mostly, how did they *feel* when they saw him? Maybe they were in love like I was, maybe they were desperate, maybe they didn't care, so long as they got to leave behind their ordinary, poor lives. But for all the varieties, the one thing they shared: the same tragic end of fulfilling his torturing voracious need—my constant vacillation between having survived and being culpable by association only aggravated by each additional demise. And I begged and pleaded to that holy power that I was unworthy of entreating: *Please let it end soon, I don't know how much more I can take.*

After some time he mentioned a young girl he met: a beautiful miller's daughter. But he was cautious with her, wanting to make a good impression and even ask for her hand. As he described her, I thought I saw a familiar hint of softness in his eyes, talking as though she was a prize to be preciously handled. And he did calm down for a while, so much so that I even wondered if he'd finally decided to repent—the hope inside me using any opportunity to rear its small head.

Until the day that everything changed. It was late afternoon and I was tidying down in the cellar—their preferred space, it turned out—when I sensed someone approaching; far too gentle to be him or one of his rowdy partners in crime. A girl appeared in the doorway.

Could you tell me if my fiancé lives here?

For a moment I thought I was dreaming. Round face, blond straw-colored hair cascading down her shoulders, green eyes and dainty mouth, and I was looking at a reflection of myself. And I knew instantly that I could not let this happen to her—for she was different. She who'd bravely ventured on her own to his lair when no one else had ever dared. It was clear by her cautious gait and resistance at being there—innocent yet aware: she'd sensed his ways without even knowing it. A nearly forgotten feeling surged through me, a joy I hadn't felt in so, so long, and I resolved I'd not let it slip away again. So I ignored the budding second-guessing calling for restraint, for I knew she'd be the one to do the thing I could not. In that moment it was decided: I'd have to help her.

Tonight when they're asleep we'll escape. I've been waiting so long for this chance.

As if on cue, our moment of resolution was cut short as we heard them drunkenly returning, dragging another bleeding girl in the midst, begging for her life as his friends started stabbing away.

She was strong, his bride-to-be, for she witnessed it all, hidden behind the wine barrel, silent as the grave as the poor victim was forcibly intoxicated until her heart burst, then had her limbs chopped and sprinkled with salt. Soon they'd passed out, as I'd given them wine laced with a sedative herb, and she came out of hiding visibly shaken. Cautiously, she stepped over the bodies as I led her upstairs to make our escape out of this den of hell.

Cloaked by the night, we ran for our lives, each step taking us out of the clouded prison and closer to our freedom. Her discernment saving us—scattered peas and lentils—leading the clear path home outlined by her precautions; having listened to the inner voice that said, *You're going to need it later.* The widened gap between he and I, and I realized there was no going back—the stretch of years that blurred all memories, my life before him like a faded dream. Her determination giving her wings, she turned around to check on me, making sure I had strength to follow her to our salvation. Eventually the mists cleared, the sunlight piercing like illuminating, protective blades, and we sighed in relief as we reached the mill, and all things would be set right again.

It was so like him to be overconfident: he'd never had any reason to be anything less. And soon he was there, eager to play the part of the perfect man, accompanied by his band to woo his supposed beloved. For the first time I truly enjoyed being the silent observer, veiled by a crowd he'd never imagine I'd be a part of. My heart pounded as she craftily played the game: coaxed by them to share her nightmare—her terrible lifelike visit to his home—gradually exposing the details of their crimes to all those present to commemorate what should've been a happy event.

I loved her—would glorify her always for the beautiful angelic essence of her being; her undeniable strength at doing what's right, so pure despite her experience. Such focus on her goal, so resolute in her convictions that life could be that simple. And though part of me wanted to defend him, still after all this time, I loved her for pronouncing the words that would seal his end, freeing me of the burden.

I liked watching him realize he was trapped; instantly seized by the town magistrate as he protested, *You don't understand—it wasn't me!* But all the same: dragged to the scaffold, noose slipped around his neck, pushed into the abyss as he dangled, struggling for breath, his toes trying in vain to reach the earth below. And I approached out of hiding if only to confirm it was really happening; that she and I were both witnessing his ultimate battle, at last released from his evil grip. His wild glare rapidly fluttered back and forth between us, as if to detect his ultimate betrayer. Gargling as he choked, his legs gave a final jolt, his large protruding dark eyes locked, fixated on me—and it was over for him. Transfixed, I waited; unsure if relieved or disappointed that his would be such a quick ending.

She smiles in accomplishment, breathing in the fresh air because for her the future is so clear—and she deserves it. And I wish I could feel as satisfied as she does, because my freedom is not like hers, not when you've been involved for so long. And though part of me longs for my previous face—for life was so different back then—I can't deny that the one I have has kept me safe in many ways. The bittersweet way time makes us get attached, catching us unaware.

So what does it matter what I look like; if I stay in this old body or return to my younger one, when ultimately none will shield me from pain? Who knows when I'll be ready to transform again—maybe in a month, a few years, perhaps never again.

Opening another door: one whose perfect timing will blur the image of his penetrating eyes from my dreams, still hungry for the one heart he consumed without destroying.

MARYAM OF THE WOODS

Sometimes I wonder if she thinks of me, until I catch myself and realize it probably intrudes on her precious freedom. Busy, independent woman with lots to do, and like a good selfless mother she's already sacrificed enough for me. Not least of all carrying me under her heart for nine months—the audacity on my part. As if I'd invaded and commanded her as a preborn spirit to yield to and serve me—as if I'd even want that power if granted it.

Perhaps it's fitting, for when I think of her I have my own lingering share of reluctance. When I was a child she was often elsewhere and, as I eventually found, more so in mind than body, so that my sadness and hurt at her cold preoccupied distance made me try my best to stay out of her way.

Don't wander far, you could get kidnapped.

But why would anyone else want that burden of me around them... And yet, most surprisingly, that didn't always sound so bad.

So off I went, to the nearby Germanic woods that were the Black Forest, the Bois de la Cambre once part of the Ardennes, or Compiègne, or some other imagined timeless garden. Then, as now, I love it all: the morning chill that transforms with the sun; the smell of pine trees and wet grass; the soothing calls of doves and cheerful chirping birds... There, countless protective trees embrace and welcome me to their ancient mysteries and tales, and no two days are ever exactly the same, yet equally rewarding in their gentle loving way. And somehow, every time, my dejection of being alone and pushed away like an unwanted weight vanished the deeper I went. That's how I knew that it was the one place where nothing bad could happen—no, not in my favorite place in the whole world.

I always held back my laughter when she told me stories of children lost in the woods amidst lurking danger. Danger, in the forest? Ignorant as I was, I sensed that had to be her creation and another way of trying to keep me close and under her control. I saw only the teeming life, both visible and hidden, beckoning to me with knowing airs at every corner—a gentle dove, a bouncy playful hare, a curious red fox, a majestic wolf, a wise Ardennais stallion—confirming that they are gentler than us. These inviting uncomplaining guardians left me wondering which animal I'd most want to be and where I'd want to live. If an angel could grant me the ability, I'd happily be a different creature every day so I could know every nook and cranny of the beautiful forest.

Innocently I easily dismissed her warnings. After all, with all the time I spent there I knew the woods better than most, and if anyone was to fear it was those who were strangers in it, not me.

Then came that day that I'll never forget.

I'd gone on a new path, east of the winding blue-green stream and further than I'd ever ventured, and though at first I couldn't see it, I knew it was there from the aroma, like something unknown and delicious was cooking. I followed the warm scent and pushed back the massive yet curiously pliable branches, until I stopped in my tracks.

There stood a cottage amidst a breathtaking emerald clearing and trees of blossoming ruby red roses. Abundant, quiet, and peaceful, the sun rays beamed straight onto the abode to the faint symphony of heavenly birds. This unexpected sight of such a blessed comforting home so moved me that I was at once filled with indescribable happiness and sorrow.

Straightening myself, I went on quietly to the nearest beckoning window and peeked inside at wondrous new things: wood carvings and bright tapestries mimicking nature in shades of magenta, red, green, and cream, along with glass teacups and ceramic bowls adorned with floral designs. My stomach gnawed at the dazzling ample sugared pastries in moon and square shapes, until a voice sent a shiver down my spine.

I turned to the woman whose soft voice and accent I couldn't place but somehow sounded familiar. The young beauty eyed me with a kind smile and green eyes deeper than my mother's. She had sun-kissed skin and her long ebony braid had strands of red and cream cloth woven through it. Draped over her shoulder, the braid seemed to flow naturally into her matching cream dress with floral motifs, against which she held a basket at her hip.

I was speechless. Where had she come from? Why hadn't I seen her before? But even if I could speak I couldn't ask such things so soon. From her clothing I could tell she was from somewhere else, maybe even a far-off magical place, and from the way she inquisitively yet warmly tilted her head I had the strangest urge to cry. She smiled and reached into the basket and handed me a ruby flower and what looked like a brown dried mass of branches curled into a ball.

"Would you like this?" she said.

I nodded, selfishly touched and happy that I'll have a Damask rose after all. "But what is that?"

"That's Kaf Maryam, a true rose of Jericho from the mustard family. My name is also Maryam."

"Like the mother of Jesus?" I said cautiously.

"I hope so," she chuckled. "You're welcome inside, if you'd like."

I carefully slipped the roses in my pocket and followed her in. Wide-eyed, I took in the musky citrus scent reminiscent of the priest at church engulfing us in aromatic clouds as he swung his censer. The plates of pastries on the polished wooden table added their spiced sweetness to the air, and with renewed conflict I imagined that it would make just as sweet a scene with the fireplace roaring in winter. I wanted to ask so many things but I didn't know where to begin.

"Curious, I see," said Maryam, and I looked away shyly. "That's good; it means you want to learn." She gestured for me to sit at the table across from her. "What do you want to know?"

"Where are you from? And when did you get here? And what about your family?" I said, trying not to sound too eager.

Her brow flickered as she looked away.

"I'm sorry, I didn't mean to pry," I said, dreading that I'd have to leave for already having gone too far.

"No, you're not," said Maryam, and when she looked up at me again, her eyes shone so brightly that I hoped it was from joy rather than restrained tears.

"I am from the land called Holy, where our God walked in earthly body. My family is all gone now, but He told me to come here, that some of these forests would remind me of home and that I'd be safe, until I'm called back again."

"So you're here alone?"

"In a sense. But I'm not the only one who had to flee; such is every war story, so it's important to remember that each day is a blessing. As the book of Ezekiel says: I will make a covenant of peace with them and rid the land of wild beasts so that they may live in the desert and sleep in the forests in safety. I love this verse from the Bible," said Maryam.

I was both shocked and a little relieved to hear that she was alone, for it selfishly suggested that I might see her again.

"How long have you been here?"

"Not too long. You could say I'm a newcomer."

"How long will you be here?"

"I don't know. But for the moment, I'm not in a hurry to go." She brought together on the table a Kaf Maryam ball-shaped dried rose and a nearby pot with small wooly green leaves and white flowers. "I like to think I'm a bit like this unusual rose whose seeds can stay dormant for years, but gradually revives with some blessed water, and even more fully with soil. That's why it's also called a resurrection plant," she smiled.

"What's Kaf Maryam mean?"

"It means Maryam's hand, after different legends around the plant. Some say that while traveling towards Nazareth, the Virgin Mary quenched her thirst with its contained water, and that her grateful blessing of it made it immortal. Others say that when Jesus was born all plants of this species thrived, or even that the plant once bloomed but since his bodily death it dries and revives to reflect the resurrection."

My brow rose. "Are you're sure it's allowed for me to have one?"

"Of course. Perhaps you're a bit like it, too," said Maryam, and I loved the pleasant feeling that she didn't seem to shrink from what she saw in me. "At least having these plants here remind me of home and keep me company, and I hope they will for you, too."

I nodded as a sense of conflict grew within me.

"I have to go now," I said reluctantly.

"It was nice to meet you, I hope to see you again."

"Would that be ok?" I said before I could stop myself.

"Yes, that's why I wanted to be sure you knew it," said Maryam. "Would you like some pastries for the road?"

"Next time," I said, wanting to display some disciplined restraint to her as much as myself.

"We'll be here," she said, and this time I grinned then left her with a happily awkward wave of the hand.

Predictably, when I got home I almost wished I'd stayed away longer.

Where have you been, spoiled girl? There's work to be done here, mother snickered.

"Like what? I thought we're not supposed to like being homemakers and cleaning, sewing, cooking and other such things because it's demeaning," I said in my most innocent tone.

Though I wasn't one to talk back, her sharp stare confirmed my response wasn't what she'd expected.

Kicking, always kicking me, just like the boy you were in my belly. Maybe it is time you grew up and found someone, though I don't know who'd be interested.

I didn't think she meant Maryam and though I only had a vague sense of what she meant, my discomfort added to the unpleasantness.

"So I'll be by myself, then," I managed after my initial stunned sadness. To add to that, maybe we both already knew then that I'd go alone before I ran off with anyone, and maybe somehow that's what upset her most. "If you came with me sometimes you'd see how nice the forest is, with all the discoveries to make. I met a young woman named Maryam—"

Maryam? That's—. She scoffed, her mean smirk lost in the distance. *Well, whoever came up with that name has some imagination. Lord knows these people can only live around their own culture, and even that's a challenge,* she said with increasingly jerky motions.

"She gave me some roses. Do you want to see?" I said, thinking I'd gift them to her if she liked them.

Roses? Ha! Like I need your childish toys. No, I have my own things to do, without whining interruption. So run along to your silly games that are more important.

I turned away, full of the familiar ugly feeling that little could satisfy her except shaming and arguing. What had I done wrong? She wanted her space and not to be bothered by me, but then when I tried to do just that she had to make me feel like I wronged her somehow. I shrank away into bed, with the roses in a shallow pot of water floating next to me like new angelic friends.

Since that's the way she wanted it, I resolved not to mention Maryam again unless she asked. There was a part of me that liked it better that way anyways, who wanted to keep Maryam to myself. I knew the tales of witches and shapeshifters who tricked children and people into trusting them, so I wasn't entirely off my guard. But I wasn't afraid and even drawn to Maryam and her serene abode full of pastries, colors, smells and miraculous stories I wanted to know more about. I could always get back to being by myself in the woods if or when I needed to.

I returned to her cozy place for the second time, and instead of me intruding, it's like she'd been expecting me all along. There were even more pastries and fresh flatbread and dishes that set my stomach grumbling.

"May you eat to your heart's content," said Maryam, gesturing to her full table that seemed out of a fairy tale.

And so I did, and the more I ate the more she seemed touched and relieved. I thought she'd grow impatient with my constant wish to identify all the deliciousness—falafel, hummus, tabbouleh, baba ganoush, and a variety of meatballs and vegetable sauces—but she seemed to love informing as much as I did discovering.

The more I ate the more my shame vanished at the thought of telling her that we often didn't have much food to eat, much less such delicious fare, but it's as though she already knew it. In the midst of my feasting a majestic white cat jumped upon the bench next to me. He politely eyed me, so that I gave him some dried tilapia that he promptly accepted.

"Noor is usually shy, but he appears to those he approves of," chuckled Maryam.

"I can see why he'd want a taste of this delicious fish," I smiled.

"Who could resist sun-dried tilapia, all the way from Galilee."

"Could that be the fish that Jesus ate?" I said, wide-eyed.

"I hope so," she said, and I mirrored her pensive smile.

For dessert I had pastries filled with dates, pistachios and other nuts, and I tried red, pink, and orange rose jams. I knew I may never taste these foods again so I couldn't resist having more of them than I normally would have.

"Some Kaf Maryam tea for eased digestion," said Maryam, pouring us each a cup, and I marveled once more at this humble plant she'd gifted me.

Eventually Maryam asked if I wanted to share about my own life, and I told her the little sad bit of it: of my father who'd gone before I was old enough to know him (and hadn't returned), and of my mother's peculiarities and I being the only child. School was too far away so I rarely went, and I had few friends mostly because my mother didn't want anyone around and they were too far for me to visit. Maryam listened to me with such a pained air on her celestial sun-kissed face that I almost started crying.

"Are you so very lonely?" she said.

"Sometimes," I shrugged. "But other times I'm not, and it's like I know that there's more, like when I'm happy in the forest, and that it's only lonely when I'm with her. And I wish I could show her that so she would be happier," I bit my lip.

"You're wise beyond your years, and she knows it, at least," said Maryam as if to herself. "Do you want to know something? You're the first person I've talked to since I've been here. I'm happy that you found me and I want you to know that you can always come here."

Deep down in my heart that's exactly what I'd wished from the moment I'd first seen the place. It seemed too good to be true when I already had the forest, but I realized her home was even better than what I'd always wished for. It may have been selfish, but I couldn't resist wishing that Maryam might be like another mother to me. At first I felt guilty for thinking this, as if it was disrespectful to my own mother's efforts, but the constant sense of being unwanted and a nuisance fueled my reasoning.

Swept into Maryam's caring world, I spent increasingly more time there so that I was hardly home at all. We read the Bible together and discussed its marvelous passages, and she told me of folk tales from the Holy Land and its surroundings. She also recited sad events from the days of early Christianity, like the massacre of Christians by Samaritans in Jerusalem and in Najran in Arabia in the sixth century; the violence that launched the medieval Crusades, the 19th century massacres in Aleppo, Jeddah, and Diyarbakir and other such conflicts, all the way up to her painful expulsion from her beloved birthplace.

"Some people say we don't exist, but they say the same thing about Jesus," said Maryam with a far-off gaze.

Though she was even more alone than me, she had a beauty and strength that I also wanted to have, and hoped she could teach me. But just her presence was enough to make the difference and made me wish all the more that my own mother would change.

One day I decided I would try once more.

"Why don't you come with me to meet Maryam," I said.

Who?

"I told you about her, she lives in the woods. You would like her, and we could be like a family."

My head instantly spun from the violence of her hand hitting my face, sending me falling to the floor.

Who are you to say what is family? As if I don't do everything already!

I rubbed my pulsing face as the tears came pouring out of me. She had never hit me before; in fact she'd always loved to brag to others about her way of disciplining me with a mere slap to the hand.

Don't you know what's happened there? They say a woman lived there who poisoned her husband, then fed his flesh in pastries and other tasty dishes to unsuspecting visitors. It must be her who's still there, a reject from the world, and now she's made you a possessed witch just like her!

I wanted to say so much, but I could only let the tears stream down my face as her icy words reached for me like a net, not only wanting to trap me but enjoying every moment of my pained torment. Though I'd suspected it before, at that moment I finally knew that something was terribly wrong; something I—and shockingly, maybe even someone like Maryam—was not meant to resolve. Sniffling, I stood up and backed away.

"Aren't you tired of always being so mad? And since I'm so bad why don't you get someone else to help?" I yelled.

For the first time in my life, she seemed stunned and was silent for a while. Her gaze took that dazed quality as she turned away, mumbling over and over: *You know nothing, nothing, nothing*—to herself, me, and someone else.

I did not sleep that night, so fearful was I that I'd find her breathing over me while I slept, like she'd done when I was a small child. The memory of being awakened by her breath on my face remains among the strangest. When at last I heard her deep snores, I moved like a ghost and gathered my few things in the darkness lit by a generous moonlight. I didn't think of him often but it suddenly occurred to me that if that was part of the reason for my father's departure, I couldn't blame him.

I left her the Damask and Kaf Maryam roses, with a note in my best handwriting of the Bible verse John 3:14. She might think me a witch, but then she'd have to explain that I not only write, but enjoy wrapping myself—and her, if she would only let me—in biblical verses.

I flew through the forest and found Maryam's cottage with its glowing candle in the windowsill, lighting the way. How easy she made it look to cast away all darkness!

Noting my red cheeks and eyes, Maryam dabbed my face with a warm cloth scented with rose water and other soothing herbs.

"I'm never going back, no matter what anyone says," I said, breaking the sad silence.

"Are you sure? It's still your family and it might get better."

"No, I wanna go; I've always been alone anyway," I sniffled.

Maryam nodded with pained understanding, she who had no one left. "We stay together then, until in His will we meet them again," said Maryam, and I fell into her strong arms and rained more bitter tears into her dress's red *tatreez* floral embroidery.

It didn't have to be like this, and yet I've never regretted my decision. Who was I to pass on a miracle that He put my way? For it could be nothing else when even through my childish innocence I perceived that I was so helpless and isolated that my prospects hardly looked promising. I still dread to even think of what else could've come from staying. Maybe I would've become even worse than her—and if I am, then at least we're no longer in each other's way, and our separation diminishes each of our dark leanings in a better way.

Still, sometimes I vacillate between delighting and feeling torn for living to write this story, even if writing often feels more like listening to spirits talking than doing a physical activity. But either way, the story exists, and it called to me to give it a physical form if only to honor the only light that will ever rescue me from darkness. As we only have one birth mother, despite my bond with Maryam I've never forgotten her, though sometimes I doubt I can say the same about her with me—and I'm learning to forgive her for it.

Maryam stayed with me and I stayed with her when we went to her holy homeland where our God had wise kings kneeling to his baby form, was loved for his knowledge and miracles, until He wasn't and died a cruel death for us all. On days when I doubt the depth of human love, I have Him and Maryam to remind me of how real, loyal, and expanding it is, and of all the loving life that endures despite the deaths. Though we did not stay there and have since made many other places our home, in a way it matters less when it perpetually lives in our souls.

I often hold the Bethlehem wood carving that Maryam gave me of the Virgin Maryam with baby Jesus in her arms, and I sometimes imagine that it's my natural mother who's finally gratefully giving me that longed-for safe, motherly embrace.

Then I humbly tear up and shrink even more when I remember that it's the infant Jesus who holds us all.

THE CONSTANT BUILDING

BRUSSELS, WINTER

I.

The building is yours.

That's what Monsieur M said. The sharply suited—and massive—dark-haired man with piercing eyes stood before me, waving official papers ready for signature if I accepted. Naturally, I was surprised; there were so many questions that needed answering. But the more I tried the more it came back to the same thing: it was all taken care of, there was no payment involved, but I had to live in it, and given the limited time he needed an answer right away. If I didn't take it, it would be torn down. Such a drastic measure so shocked me that I almost asked if no one else wanted it, but something in me refrained, not wanting to question what seemed like strange luck.

To add to that, there was an alluring intensity about the man, who didn't seem the kind to be disobeyed. But even as that impression came over me, I wasn't in the least bit afraid. Instead I was pleasantly amused by his strong presence, like beneath that serious, no-nonsense manner was a toughness derived from affectionate care rather than love of violence.

As for the question at hand: the towering, multi-floored historic property had always fascinated me. It was located in Rue de Flandre, in the narrow 11th century street in the Porte de Flandre, right by Boulevard de Nieuport and the Bruxelles-Charleroi canal. From our childhood walks, I recalled its dark old stone looking down on us small souls with all the bearing of its age. I had a vague memory of the street being part of an ancient trade route that ran through Brussels from east to west.

Each time we passed by, I heard the cries of children coming from behind its opaque double-swing metal gates, making me peek through the thin space between them to decipher their shapes happily stomping on the asphalt. It also had its peculiarities, like the impression that the building faced the wrong way, at least compared to every other structure around it. To enter you'd have to push the heavy loud gates, step into the courtyard, and enter to the left, when all the other buildings faced south out on to the street. What's more, it looked as if nestled behind these other buildings, and despite towering above them, its large fence added to its cloistered yet ever pervading air.

Despite my lingering curiosity, that's all it ever was: a mysterious building I only saw from outside, that I associated with happiness, and at times a bit intimidating air; a place meant for a selected few unlike myself.

So while I had no idea what I'd specifically do with the building, I knew instantly, without a shred of a doubt that I didn't want it demolished. Just the concept seemed downright sacrilegious, and I loved that these realizations rushed at me then all at once, when I'd never given them much thought before that moment.

Before I even uttered the words, the charismatic smirking visitor extended the papers to me, like he knew all along that I'd agree. After signing, he handed me a vintage leather portfolio decorated with vine leaves, filled with a filigree-decorated metal key and dossier with some information, whose quick skimming revealed no contact details.

Don't worry, we're never very far, said Monsieur M without my asking, flashing a pearly smile, and vanished as quickly as he'd appeared.

Dazed, I dropped on my small couch in my small studio in the small grey Molenbeek street I lived in, wondering what I'd just done. I was already struggling to make ends meet, wondering each day how I'd manage another, and now to add to this—until I recalled that this building didn't involve any payment. I almost laughed: how hadn't I questioned him on this? It's like he'd taken advantage by hurrying me with the time constraint.

But if it was a lie then how could I be held accountable; I could then change my mind, tell the authorities to take it back, and I'd be free of it... And back to what? To more of this? Whatever *it* entailed couldn't be so bad, and if I wanted answers it seemed clear that I had to go there myself, and the sooner the better. My reasoning combined with a few Leonidas pralines—the sweet small luxuries that lessen the stings of uncertainty—helped reassure me.

Thus I was swept away, for try as I might to ignore it, I was curious; my resurging childhood memories making me giddy with innocent happiness. I realized that I could hardly recall when I'd last seen it—it had been that long. An urgency filled me to see it again and compare its actual state to the way I remembered it, and fill in the voids with confirmed forms. Yet more than see, I could and would *live* there—at least after making sure it was safe and as stated—and I could actually finally leave this place, when I'd so often wanted nothing else.

Somewhat unconsciously, I started packing, not that I had much to pack anyway. My most prized possessions were a few carefully packed old outfits—no mere "dress-up" for me when they held too much historical meaning—and, of course, my books. While I'd learned to downsize over the years, the one thing that likely wouldn't decrease, or by much, were my books. My heart jumped at the thought of all the space I'd finally have to fit them all in properly, with more to come, in that new abode.

It dawned on me that I'd even quit my job, not because I no longer wanted or needed to work, but because I was tired of relying on the illusion of safety granted by a semi-predictable paycheck and that, crazy as it sounded, these new circumstances might allow me to do something else. As any Christian is aware of the rebelliousness continuously in the air, perhaps it only added to the defiance after the events of C20. Many had lost their jobs and if all was going to hell anyway, why not try something else or at least try to reasonably enjoy oneself? If I knew one thing, it was that all kinds of jobs would always be there, and though working some may not fit one's dream or ideal, it didn't make it any less a reflection of one's dedication or talent. I could at least try—surely there had to be a reason behind this—and it shocked me that for the first time the uncertainty didn't seem as intimidating as before.

Though I initially thought I'd wait a few days—I had to plan how to move my stuff there—the next day I dismissed everything and decided to go straight there. I hardly slept the night before, my nervous excitement making me wish I could just take everything with me to leave on the spot.

A glance through my large messenger bag comforted me: wallet with cash, cell phone and charger, a notebook and pens. Pepper spray and a blade, which I'd never resorted to and hoped would remain unused. Tucked in furthest, nestled in the buoyant, organized mess was an acacia box, adorned with a cross at center and vines around it. There was a bittersweet solace to having learned from my parents at a young age to always keep the essentials close to me, in case I'd ever have to leave quickly.

The *Métro* ride was a blur as my mind filled with new possibilities and ideas, of how this had come together, and what could come of it. It was a big building, and though I loved—needed—the quiet, did I really want to be there alone all the time? Even with all my books there would be extra space that could perhaps be put to other use. My stomach squeezed in an unpleasant knot. What if I failed and was left alone?

But just as quickly it seemed to clear, and I knew that it wasn't what unsettled me; it was this *new* thing, whatever *it* was, the potential dangers of the unknown. As if constant, familiar discomfort was any less horrifying. I welcomed this cheerful, logical aspect to my cautious side in the midst of such change.

I arrived at the Rue de Flandre stop and waded through the station, feeling curiously different after all this time. The crowds diminished as I followed my exit, and emerged above into the foggy boulevard along the canal. I remained fixed in place: much was as I remembered it, and a stillness I hadn't expected filled the space. I glanced a remodeled café at center of the boulevard that brought memories of past visits, flanked on the right by the wide Rue Antoine Dansaert, and at left by my Rue de Flandre. Suppressing my frown, I tried to reassure myself that my memory was playing its faithful part in contrasting unfamiliar changes.

Leaving behind industrial Molenbeek, I crossed the bridge and veered left, my steps slowing to take in all the details. A variety of grey and reddish-brown buildings towered over me, the quiet as if more concentrated for its tighter space. The bakery at right was still there, beckoning with its tasty *mattentaart* cakes, Liège waffles, cuberdon candies shaped in triangular priest's hat, and other sweets. A few steps down and to the right was the short Rue de la Clé, connecting to the parallel Rue Antoine Dansaert.

Gratitude filled me to be granted the experience of living at an entrance point to the beloved *centre ville,* the heart of the city with its church Sainte Catherine, church Saint Nicolas, la *Grand Place*, and the Cathedral of Saints Michel and Gudule, dedicated to the city's patron saints. Any small loft anywhere would've been a blessing, but now I was to be in a large historic building that conveniently looked away from the many bland, block-like factory buildings of the Molenbeek we grew up in. Here was the happy winding path that led to all the delights of the city center and *la Grand Place*, that as a child I was too young to know were already starting to shift in unpleasant ways.

Saving it for last, I looked up to the left, and there it was: the same tall, dark chocolate brown building, towering behind a new though similarly protective fence. I began digging through my bag for the key, until a slight nudge of my arm against the fence made it tilt back in open invitation. I slipped in and finally, for the first time, took in the fullness of the courtyard.

The vast, rectangular space had faded white crayon drawings of *marelle* grids on the asphalt, and blue, yellow, and lavender sketches of flowers, birds, and stick-figured forms. A subtle laughter echoed, but I sensed it'd been a while since anyone had played there. For a moment I wondered about these past children: if they were adults, still living in Belgium, or gone elsewhere, maybe never to return? Did they still think of this place sometimes, and hopefully happily? I reflected on the bittersweet peculiarities of our movements through space. Could we cling to precious memories, no matter how brief, enough to make us leave a part of ourselves there to more easily return at will? There was a kindness to knowing that sometimes we returned to them in unexpected ways, and I was once more overcome with gratefulness that this place should have miraculously come into my hands.

With reverent emotion I turned to my new home, its fogged up massive tree-like form disappearing into the mist above.

You are a mist that appears for a little while and then vanishes—I smiled as the Bible verse of James 4:14 resonated in my thoughts, easing me of a burden with its gentle reminder that I don't know what tomorrow will bring. The brick walls were dotted with long windows that made up the lower *rez de chaussée* and three upper floors. I glanced at a window to the far right on the first floor, frowning at my odd sense that its window was cracked—who would dare!—but was only an optical illusion.

My heart racing as I stood before the pair of thick wooden doors painted green, I slid the old key through the lock, and with a clink of grinding metals and some pushing, the doors yielded. As my immediate surroundings lit up with the incoming light, I beheld the hazy hallway, the stagnant air urging me to throw open the doors to aerate. I flipped the light switch, and thankfully the place was enrobed in a soft light, neither a sickening old yellow nor too bright.

One of the marvels of this and other European cities, was the propensity for locations to look small from the outside, but surprisingly spacious once inside. Though I already anticipated all the added space it would surely have, its extent surpassed what I imagined, and seemed almost contradicting what was seen at mere first glance. The hardwood floor hallway—whose beautiful wavy grain suggested Bethlehem olive wood—stretched ahead, with doors at each north and south sides that revealed offices with old desk and dressers, but were otherwise empty of anything else. Despite the building's age—late 19th to early 20th century, I guessed—everything was well-kept, with new renovations blurring the lines between past and present. I kept the pattern of opening the windows as I went through each room, marveling at how many people such a place could hold.

I came to the end of the hallway with an equally appealing wooden staircase at right. With all there was to see, I decided to begin with the top floor and work my way down. I knew enough about the paranormal and haunted houses not be one of those who only did the minimum and ignored everything else, only to later find that there was something dwelling up there they could've found sooner if only they'd checked. In comic contrast, I wasn't expecting to find treasures the likes of the Brussels hoard of 1908 full of medieval coins, but I didn't mind that some things were starting to feel delightfully less impossible.

I climbed the stairs, my fingers grazing the banister as my cautious steps made the only light sound on the sturdy wood. Thankfully, the stuffiness decreased the further up I went. A sweet musky scent grew stronger, reminding me of frank and myrrh. At the top, third landing, the hallway stood between myself and the first door before me.

I entered and stared, awestruck for a few moments by the contents answering my mounting concerns. A small box with a few lights embodied the latest installed Wi-Fi system that radiated throughout the building.

The fastest service, guaranteed! I read its sticker with a smile.

Curiously, this latest technology contrasted a large olive wood set-up on the wall, holding three rows of bronze bells, each coupled with its own cord. I pulled on the one that I assumed would be the room immediately below me and heard a reverberating bell ring below, vibrating the ground along with the whole place. I repeated the motion, confirming that this old-fashioned way of ringing directly into each room seemed an effective back-up emergency communication of sorts.

I glided to the back of the room, where a range of cameras and flat screens revealed a high quality security system. Not only was the building secure and able to alert authorities if trespassing points were triggered, but the cameras had a bird's eye view of the vicinity that could zoom out over the whole city.

Activate, read one of the switches. I contemplated flipping it, if only to see what it would do, but decided to leave it for later. A separate screen showed a similar system that allowed for not just national, but global monitoring of potential alarming situations.

Increasingly impressed, whatever worries I had about the location's safety were quickly put to rest. Although a useful unexpected find, even for a previous school, I wondered if it was really necessary. Still, I was always one for the adage of *Better safe than sorry*. It also pleasantly contrasted from what some would deem the building's dated look, and this addition to its air of ancient knowledge pleased me. Amused, I held back from stirring awake some of the black screens, half imagining that my info would pop up on a screen—the all-knowing elder building having done its fruitful research on the person who would come and stand right where I was.

With a peculiar satisfaction I proceeded east to the rest of the floor, discovering a series of quaint studios adorned in white and gold paint. The equally charming full bathrooms with showers caught my attention, for they'd clearly been a recent addition. Each room smelled as peacefully inviting as the next, and seemed perfect living spaces for any resident.

I descended to the second floor, host to a large kitchen and eating hall. Its olive wood cabinets were fully stocked with packaged beans and legumes, with granite counters covered in overflowing bowls of fresh fruit, and the refrigerator packed with fresh vegetables, eggs, and various breads. Even the freezer had ample pike and carp fish, meat, and mouthwatering *boudin*, *frikadel* and *merguez* sausages reminiscent of tasty Belgian *fritures*.

Emotion overcame me: I'd recently decided to do my best to eat as healthy as I could, even if it meant paying more and eating less, at least it would pay off in quality and help keep me in good health. I knew all about having to make do, so it was just a matter of managing this readjustment. I sent a thought of thanks to Monsieur M for providing more than the basic needs that wouldn't make a dent in my modest resources.

Most unexpected was the tall cabinet in a corner filled with spirits. I was struck by the poster inside of the 1958 Brussels Expo and memorabilia of Brasserie Vandenheuvel's Ekla Pils, that beer deemed the star of the show and could be enjoyed at the new Atomium. It had also been an occasion for Vandenheuvel to celebrate its hundred-year legacy, whose roots went back to the city center as the Brasserie Saint Michel, until their expansion and name change brought them to Molenbeek. Despite the Expo 58 success, it was temporary and less than two decades later the brewery was closed down.

I pinched a smile at the bygone history, recalling how often I'd walked down Rue Edmond Bonehill and stared up at the ghostly vacant Vandenheuvel building. With its appealing eclectic 1920s architecture that made me think of old movie venues, its geometric Art Deco-like wrought iron gates, and floating skybridge, I defiantly decreed that it had to always remain in place.

There were also plenty of fruity gueuze lambics—that Brussels Champagne—and I almost gasped when I saw the red-colored *liqueur de rose*. I'd looked all over for the sweet rose liquor ever since I'd first tasted it as a child, to no avail. It may have been my imagination but the bottles before me may have even been of the same exact brand as the one I'd first tasted so long ago. Last but not least were the white, rosé, and red wines. Though there were some from all over the world, it was the Middle Eastern wines that most caught my attention. Despite my inability to read their foreign labels, I recognized many flags that inspired a familiar, nostalgic longing.

The vast kitchen space also had a large stove and oven, and I smiled to imagine people here cooking a big feast, and even if it was a rare thing, it was nice to know it was possible.

I went down to the first floor, which consisted of twelve classrooms, six on each north and south sides, with about forty wooden desk and chairs in each, making for a decently sized school. The classic dark green chalkboards with the newly installed flat screens delighted me once more. In a way, they reflected my own wavering between old and new, and for all the benefits of—and necessity for—new technology, I often found comfort in stepping away from it.

As I exited the last classroom, I noted the adjacent room with a pair of reddish-brown cedar doors that differed from all the others, so I deduced it might be some kind of office, perhaps where the instructors held meetings. I pushed down the antique handle and my breath stopped: there before me was the most majestic library, filled from top to bottom with books, along with ample empty shelves for all the ones I would be adding. The teal carpet with floral designs was as inviting as the bronze antique fireplace and the two leather chairs and low table set cozily in front of it. I gravitated to the long windows facing south, granting me view out into the street below, and decided I'd begin by staying in that delightful space.

"Nice view, isn't it."

I shrieked as I turned, and unconsciously reached into my purse.

"H—how did you get in here?" I retorted. I wasn't sure what shocked me more: that the guy before me looked so at ease in the place or that his dark, brawny handsomeness was equally arresting.

"My apologies. I'm Paolo. The door was left open downstairs," he said.

Mediterranean. Of course, he would be Mediterranean.

"And so you thought it perfectly fine to just walk in here unannounced?"

His brow flickered and something in his manner made me almost feel bad.

"I'm familiar with the area, and when I saw the door open it caught my attention, so I came in. I was sure I'd be heard and though that's my mistake, I can't blame you for being absorbed in this place," said Paolo, taking steps towards me that I wasn't sure I wanted. He seemed to notice and, raising his palms, he stopped.

"Well, no, I didn't, and with all due respect, it still doesn't explain what brings you here."

"Right. I've brought all your belongings, so you can begin settling in," said Paulo with a self-satisfied smile that gave him such an innocent boyish air that I suppressed a laugh.

"Brought my belongings? But—"

"I was instructed to."

"Instructed? By whom?"

"By Monsieur M." His tone simultaneously implied that it could be no one else and hinted surprise at my ignorance.

"I see. He hadn't said anything about that."

"He assumed you'd want to move right in, so here I am. He's not usually wrong, but it would be interesting if he was this time. Was he?"

"No," I said in a near whisper.

He nodded. "So shall I bring it all here, then?"

"Yes, please."

I observed him moving the first few boxes using a dolly, aware that it would be no small feat even for a bulky guy like himself to handle what were mostly books. The weight of words—and knowledge—was no joke, but he handled the few back and forth trips up and down the stairs without complaint. And goodness, that only added to his handsomeness.

"Thank you for that, even if it's just another workout day for you," I smirked, handing him a bottle of water that he accepted.

"No thanks needed," he said with a smile. His white shirt glued to his biceps as he nearly emptied the bottle. "Browsing some of your collection was quite rewarding in itself. A lot of unique, hard-to-find titles."

Handsome and at least appreciative of books? It was getting harder to suspect him.

"Good eye. Do you like reading?"

"I do. Might I ask where these, or at least some, come from?"

"My parents had a spiritual bookstore nearby, shortly before I was born. They managed to keep some of the most precious to them. Though they split up when I was young, I like to think that love was passed on to me, because I've since acquired my own pieces, too."

"Seems like you kept the good stuff." His brown eyes bore into mine, amusing me with his flirtation. "Can't hurt to be prepared with the paranormal stuff."

"The Bible does often say to be prepared."

"Very true." Paolo laughed warmly and finished his water, while I refrained from saying that though this meeting itself smacked of the paranormal, it wasn't one I was prepared for.

"So since you seem familiar with this place, tell me about it."

His brow twitched. "What do you want to know?"

"Like what was it, how was it? I mean I assume it was some kind of school; I recall the laughing children. But today was my first time inside, after all these years of wondering."

His features darkened. "That's right, it was an elementary school. You really didn't know this?"

"No," I shrugged.

He nodded. "I see. Well I apologize again for earlier, but I have to get going," he said, as if distracted. "Thanks for the water, and no need to remind you to lock doors and activate switches to keep folks such as myself away."

"Right," I said, unsure what to say at the sudden shift. But what had I expected? It wasn't like I was going to hold him back, even as I debated if I should ask how to get hold of him, like in case any of my things were missing? I gave myself credit for that spur of the moment thought, at least, while he appeared to search through his pockets.

"Just in case, here's my number; if I can help with anything," said Paolo, somewhat avoiding my gaze as he extended his card.

"Thanks, I appreciate it," I said, and with a last smirk and wave of the hand, he was gone.

Paolo Angeli, Architect—impressive, I smirked as I held his smooth card and leisurely went to obediently lock the doors. Curious as it was, overall I deemed the encounter positive. I couldn't lie to myself that I hoped I'd see him again, and although I wasn't sure I'd reach out to him, to have his number was an added reassurance. It occurred to me that perhaps that's what Monsieur M. had intended all along. Whatever the case, I was now moved into my new home and everything was fine.

For added safety more than alarm, I went up and activated the security system, then refreshed myself with a shower in one of the studios. Then I grabbed some food and Dabouki Bethlehem red wine, and spent the evening trying to process all the last day's events as I settled in the library. Arranging your personal things always had a way of making any space feel like home, so that I felt more at ease once everything had found its place. I set my precious cross-decorated acacia box on the table, filling the space with its ancient sacred presence. There were so many books I wanted to browse through, but thought again with gratitude that I'd get to that soon. The sky had just gotten dark when I settled into my thin foam mattress by the fireplace, with my laptop and wine close at hand.

There's a pleasure to enjoying the beauty of older architecture amidst the benefits of our modern time—dissolving the spaces between time as I enjoyed the best of both worlds. I got on the internet and realized that at some point, I'd already decided, so I sent off my resignation email and closed that chapter. Maybe it was the thrill of being amidst new walls, but one thing after another, more memories surged, and along with it the urge to reach out to old and new friends, though not without fighting every inner protest that it was pointless. And so what if it was? I could still send the email; even if you can't make it it's nice sometimes to hear from old friends, let them know that you still remember the happy moments you once shared, no matter how long it's been. So I wrote, telling them of my new situation and inviting them to visit whenever they'd like, although, as usual, the older one gets the less you expect it to happen.

The deed done, I cozied into my foolproof woolen blanket and Sacha Guitry's comical gem, *"Ils étaient neuf célibataires,"* and drifted off to the Brusseleer accent of Gustave Libeau playing one of the nine bachelors.

II.

The first night in a new place is always the biggest test. The ancient dream incubators knew this, from Ancient Egypt to Late Antique Christianity. But I drifted off so quickly that I'd already seen it as a good sign. To prove it, I awoke feeling refreshed, and even with a lingering silly smile at the thought of Paolo who'd been there. The more I focused, trying to remember my dream, I vaguely recalled some sense of urgency and chaos that then merged with him. As the last part of the dream, I remembered it most, and gladly lingered in his warm, familiar energy—likely my wishful thinking, but I obviously didn't mind.

The rest of the day was quiet and relaxing, and I took so much to the new abode that I didn't even step out. With ample desserts and cups of tea available, everything I needed was conveniently there. So I immersed myself in unpacking my books and arranged a spiritual shelf with different translations of the Bible, texts by the ascetic theologian Origen of Alexandria, Cyril of Alexandria, the hymnographer Ephrem the Syrian, and other early Christian Eastern church figures. Glancing at the titles on early Christian martyrs reminded me that not even this place, often known for its tolerance, had been spared historic religious violence. I resolved that soon I'd take a walk to the nearby Church of Saint Nicholas and see the gilded reliquary of the Martyrs of Gorkum, in memory of the nineteen Dutch Catholic clerics who were hanged by Calvinists in July 1572 in Brielle for their faith.

Wishfully countering that ecumenical strife, I went on joining my volumes of Eastern Orthodox Fathers, Hildegard von Bingen, the trials of Joan of Arc, and the stigmatic Anne Catherine Emmerich. There was also Swedenborg's full inventory, with his sweeping *Arcana Caelestia* nearly commanding its own shelf, and Jakob Lorber's own impressive collection.

I then browsed the library's own collection: full of comics, novels by Germanic and Belgian authors, local legends, medieval history by Henri Pirenne, and Roman history of Gallia Belgica, whose pleasantly worn leatherbound covers beckoned with a playful air of secret knowledge. I smiled, recalling Julius Caesar's view of the Belgae—the largest tribal confederation in this area conquered during his Gallic Wars—as the bravest for being furthest from the civilization and refinement of the Romans. I pondered if his meaning of bravest really meant rebellious and unwilling to submit, and it wouldn't be the last time that I wished societies would either peacefully co-exist or leave each other alone.

After spending time learning about the medieval Stavelot, Parc Abbey, and Floreffe Bibles, I shifted to literature with Charles de Coster's classic *Ulenspiegel*, Georges Eekhoud's *New Carthage*, Rodenbach's *Bruges-la-Morte*, and Marguerite Yourcenar's *Memoirs of Hadrian*. Then

I revisited childhood memories with the comics *Astérix*, *Tintin*, the Western *Lucky Luke*, and the beloved small blue humanoid *Schtroumpfs*.

Part of the pleasure of reading is in the way you're transported elsewhere, and I so delightfully drifted that I hardly noticed a full week pass.

III.

Slowly I awoke, wallowing in a space of misty greyness so typical to Brussels, my face happily buried in my pillows.

Until I saw it from the corner of my eye.

There I lay, in an 18th century four-poster bed with teal damask and gold embroidered curtains and tassels keeping me privately warm. Cautiously I peeked through the curtains and sighed in relief at the dresser with my cross-decorated box faithfully on it. Next to it was a booklet titled *Annonces et avis divers des Pays-Bas*, printed at Rue d'Assaut, while the walls had exquisite 18th century gold-framed maps that I hadn't seen before.

Because they hadn't been there.

It's a strange thing to instantly know that you're in the same location, yet one utterly transformed by its rearranged elements. Because it was essentially the same room, but now with what looked like a late 18th century French Neoclassical style.

I went to the maps colored with green, red, and yellow, and read the name Joseph de Ferraris, 1777, with others engraved by Dupuis. One showed a full aerial view of the Habsburg Netherlands, while a larger one zoomed in to the Brussels and Porte de Flandre area I now dwelled in. I marveled at all the time and detail it must've taken, with the distinct artistic flair lacking in Google Maps.

Eager to inspect the rest of the grounds in search of answers, I grabbed the nearest coat—of navy wool embroidered with gold—trying to guess what it would all look like outside. The yard was now sturdy cobblestone that continued out into the blessedly clean street, and I beamed to see the towering building not only facing south, but with a lovely stepped gables design. Crowning it was a statue of Archangel Michael, his brandished spear pointing both to Heaven and earth.

A few steps down to the right, to what I knew as the corner of the street overlooking the canal, was the Senne River towered by the massive stone rampart of the Porte de Flandre. With its stepped gables and two dark pointy-roofed towers, it made for a medieval fortification whose walls wrapped all around the city.

"Aside from the overdue need for repairs, how do you like it?"

Something like butterflies fluttered in my stomach at the sound of Paolo's voice, and I turned to find him attired like an 18th century courtier. Had he known I'd thought of contacting him to discuss all this?

"You certainly do know when to show up," I chuckled.

"At your service," said Paolo with a light bow and hand to his heart. His shiny ebony hair was perfectly combed back in a ponytail with two rolls of curls above his ears. Even more impressive that it wasn't a wig.

"So what's going on? I mean this view nice, even bucolic in a way. But what's the occasion?" I said, looking over his navy blue and gold outfit. Decidedly he'd look handsome no matter what he wore, topped with his endearing playful easiness.

"*Devinez, mademoiselle.*"

"So my guess is it's sometime after 1777, based on the Ferraris maps."

"Right. It's 1783," he said with a conflicted air.

"Good year, with the signing of the Treaty of Paris ending the American Revolutionary War; with France, Spain, and the Dutch supporting the Americans against Great Britain," I smirked. "But wait—is something about to get destroyed?"

"Sadly, yes. We're witnessing the last of the Porte de Flandre as it stands before us. Even if it didn't prevent Louis XIV from bombarding Brussels in 1695 and Louis XV's troops from invading in 1746, I still think such walls could serve their purpose."

"I agree. Walls may not be foolproof but they can at least help better monitor and control the passage of people. In a perfect mature world I wouldn't mind open borders, but until then I distrust wild human nature that is often easier to resort to."

He nodded with a pensive air, and it touched me that he seemed to be deeply processing what I was saying. Perhaps he shared my dislike of Louis XIV's troops who'd turned Molenbeek into a battlefield, with their cannons strategically positioned towards the city center while nearby farms housed French troops. At least his successor Louis XV was sensitive enough to apologetically return the treasured Manneken Pis stolen by his invading troops, complete with a new regal outfit to go with his honorary title of Knight of the Royal and Military Order of Saint-Louis.

"I share the feeling. And as architect, a part of me likes to see a potential connection between certain values and the way our most important buildings and homes—those places where we spend so much time—look."

"Your preferred way of merging past and present, I presume," I smirked.

"Yes, whenever possible. Surely neither of us are fans of the latest modern creations," said Paolo.

"I find it entirely unappealing. May those who like it enjoy it because I can't," I said. "So what's the solution?"

"Great question. Get dressed and we'll go on our requisite 18th century revelatory nature walk and I'll explain," he said with a flirty air.

Paolo walked me back to the building and waited outside as I returned to the library, where I nearly stopped in my tracks when I saw it. I drifted to the sky blue *Robe à la Française*, with stitched gold vines and roses delicately blooming on its surface, and white Brussels lace hanging luxuriously down the elbow sleeves. It was a dress stepped out of my dreams. What *is* it about old clothes that feels like a bittersweet reunion, like I left something behind?

Somehow I managed to get comfortably into the dress without extra help, though it did occur to me that Paolo might not mind me requesting his assistance. Caught in the sight of my new self in it, I lingered in front of the mirror longer than expected, and even did a light version of my stacked hair with a few curls and white foundation make-up in the 18th century French style. It was rare that I had the opportunity to dress up in such a way and it only added to the dreamy fairy-tale quality of this experience—and all because of the building. All these years of lone searching and longing and now here it was: a sense of it all coming together somehow. I was starting to feel like—and hopefully not just wish that—the building drew people to it, when it'd had that very effect on me.

All dolled up, and leaving my skirt *panier* behind, I glided down the stairs and hall in my low curved Louis heels, laughing at the playful scene. I tried to imagine wearing this in the *Métro*, wondering how effective it would be at keeping unwanted contact at bay. At least one thing that the global C20 pandemic had accomplished was recommending—if not requiring—a certain level of distance from others, a concept I gladly support.

Paolo appeared in the doorway and stood still for a moment, staring.

"If only I could figure out whose ideas all this was," I smirked as he reached for my hand.

"Mine, of course, and I was entirely right," Paolo said, and gallantly kissed my hand that seemed so small in his. There was such an intimacy in his gentle gesture that I easily yielded to his caring guidance.

We turned right and went towards the canal at a leisure pace.

"Everything has been well here, I take it?" he said, with what I thought was a hint of unease.

"Yes, like a perfect fairy tale, actually. Even if I didn't expect to witness changes of Jules Anspach proportions," I chuckled.

"Is that a complaint? Are you missing anything?"

I loved that he seemed genuinely concerned and in a way I was, but how could I say it? "I'm grateful for what this is, even if it may not last," I said, wondering if I'd said too much.

"Do you regret coming here, accepting the building?" His dark eyes bore into me in such a way I hoped my white powder concealed it.

"Not at all. It was fast, but I'm learning that not all decisions have to take so long to make."

He nodded. "It's like it took this to happen to make you step out, in a way?"

"Yes. It even feels like the decision was made for me, but in a benevolent nonintrusive way, like a blessing."

"Monsieur M has that effect," said Paolo, and I almost added that he did too, in his own charming way.

We came to the medieval gate and walked through it, then along the bridge over the Senne River.

"May I take you on a boat ride of the Senne?" he said, gesturing to a large rowboat awaiting us.

"I'd be delighted," I said, and he helped me settle before seating himself with the oars.

He seemed so natural as he easily rowed the boat in his historic clothing that I couldn't help but smile as I gazed at him. I knew he noticed because he smiled back but distinctly avoided looking at me at times with a lingering air of pensiveness. In the distance were other rowboats with merchants and passengers from near and far. I glimpsed the road that I knew as the

Chaussée de Gand with buildings and inns for travelers, and vast farms nearby that looked so lovely I may as well have been in another country.

"I didn't know it could be so idyllic here. So then, are we going back in time—to the rivers of belief?" I said tentatively.

"In a sense, yes; revisiting the past to remember where we come from. And nice touch with the Enigma reference," Paolo grinned, making me like him even more.

"Why now?" I said, as we reached a portion of the river shaded by trees and overlooking the gate with its own Archangel Michael.

"Because," he said, letting his strong arms finally rest, "The Society of Constant Building is fast reconvening."

"That sure sounds very 18th century. Did you make it up?" I smirked and waited for him to continue.

"I thought that was clever," he chuckled. "But in spiritual principle it's always existed. By now you've noticed that with time people have drifted away from our spiritual source, down to rejecting or rewriting history, whose material source is always spiritual. But by His grace, there's always been—" He leaned into me with an alluring smile. "And there will always be those who play their part in preserving and sharing history, good and bad."

"But what would I have to do with that?"

"Don't be so surprised. The strong mind you cultivated helps you to travel in time. And your parents were part of it, too, as were mine and others, even when they're often unaware of it. Sometimes there's memories attached to objects, too. I'm guessing some of your older books and belongings might have some. It's not a coincidence that you were drawn to them; it's all connected."

I wondered if he knew about my acacia box decorated with the cross.

"And so the building was a school for?" My gaze narrowed.

"Spiritually gifted children," said Paolo. "Until they left after all the scandals; some explained and some not. Disappearance, poisoning, kidnapping, murder—I hate to think of it but our Lord handles it all."

"So that's why it's been vacant all this time," I said as sadness filled me, hating that there are evil entities that enjoy harming pure innocence.

Paolo nodded and fixed on me. "But Monsieur M knows when and how to gather us together, following the highest orders, naturally. So here we are, all called to be teachers of sorts, in our own way, as we keep learning ourselves."

I pinched a smile, recalling how I'd often been told that I'd make a great teacher but didn't think myself qualified for it.

"I reached out to let people know of my new situation, but I haven't heard back from anyone. I guess it's just me for now," I shrugged.

"Don't worry, the right ones will come in due time, maybe even your parents," he said with a suddenly tense air. "And that's where—" he cleared his throat. "I hope, if you agree of course, that you might allow me to be there, to help you in any way I can."

"Like—"

"Kindred souls with a shared spiritual vision," said Paolo quickly.

"I would like that," I said humbly.

His awkward chuckle only made him sweeter. "And maybe in time this friendship could become—something more."

"That's what I was hoping for," I said with my best smile and what had to be our joined pounding hearts.

Paolo exhaled and wrapped my hands in his.

"Oh, I'm so glad to hear you say this. I'd forced myself for the boat ride so that I'd have no way out," he said.

"Now I understand why you sometimes seemed so nervous. So was this Monsieur M's doing, too?"

"He knew to contact you of all people about the building, and that we would be a good match. And no matter what came of it, he assigned me to watch over you," said Paolo with an air of grateful relief.

"Right, so like my guardian angel."

"I'd like that," he said, and drew me into a kiss that I didn't want to end.

IV.

This time when I awake, I smile at the evident change.

The walls are limestone, perfect for the Middle Eastern desert heat. My heart full, I hold back happy tears at the sight of my white silk dress for our wedding day. At last, no longer alone but united with the one sent to watch over me and to share his life mission with, when I didn't know or expect it.

I'm beginning to understand why it keeps happening; this flooding of forgotten, maybe even suppressed old memories, happy but also often painful and tied to our families who had to flee. Peace in the Middle East—and the whole world, but it can only come from one holy name.

Peace I leave with you, my peace I give to you, says Jesus.

It's the sixth century in the vast Holy Land, and my cross-decorated box holding one of the earliest Bibles in Arabic is back to its birthplace. The building is a dormitory for pilgrims on the way to Jerusalem and elsewhere, but can also be a humble school, whether for children or for spiritual learning. Reinvigorated with local olive oil and wine, travelers share stories of near and far, like the first Merovingian King Clovis I of the Franks, whose kingdom stretches to Gallia Belgica. Born a pagan, he embraced Arian Christianity, then changed to Nicene Christianity with his wife's influence. Well known is Emperor Justinian's ambitious reconquering of the Western Roman Empire territory, and attempt to use alliance with Frankish kings to fight the Arian Goths. Much can be said about Justinian, but he did survive the devastating bubonic plague. Some will also say that, soon after, Gaugericus, Bishop of Cambrai, built a chapel on an island in the Zenne—the Senne River that still flows through Brussels—dedicated to Saint Michael.

Whatever the era, the building is constant, changing yet remaining, playing its part in gathering the Lord's children together in this life, and the next. In a past dream, I was in Rue de Flandre looking up at the building, turned limestone pale yellow in the late desert afternoon. A sense of quiet desolation reigned, as the side of the Ghassanid structure revealed a jagged void from a destructive blow. But it's made whole again, by Ghassanid soldiers and other faithful community residents, and the constant building will be rebuilt as often as necessary and in myriad suitable forms.

It's a beautifully sunny day, bustling with the market and merchants from near and far, some wearing trinkets of Saint Nicolas of Myra for safe travels. I beam in my dress when I hear the bells of the chapel calling me home.

THE ENTITY

Some Parallel Dimension

I like watching her come into view: her essence gradually appearing into my space—a faded, creeping shape, darkening into being, until we're in the same wavelength where she can hear me, even if she doesn't know how or why it's happening. Oh, humans; so foolish, that sometimes it's hard to feel bad that they're such easy prey. But there's something about her that drew me in—her cautious curiosity? Her frailty that compliments her innocence? The endless possibilities?—so I've been lurking for some time, easing my way in, gaining ground.

I waver in my state, alternating between the marvel that I've never been in a human body but that it will soon change. Pace accelerating, and all according to plan, for soon we'll be united as deep down she wants—I'll convince her of it. Oh, her actions prove it, and she knows but ignores it; that feeling from deep down in that black pit she likes to think can't exist—just her imagination, surely—but is oh so real. And even people around her have started commenting on it, but fancies will have their day, and I take advantage of the opportunities that come my way. Fine by me; that all signs point to her being mine, for she makes it so easy to lure her away from stopping me, so fragile, so unsure—that it must be my task to show her another way to live. So I'll wait for the right time to sneak myself in, so much so that she won't know that it's her own doing.

And for the most part, it *is*! (Just like she won't know til later that she's partially the one writing this tale.) I haven't told the others here (and I'm not sure that I will), but I'm torn between wanting to show her, tell her this, and maintaining my cover. But even my skillful duplicity is a temporary state, a step in the right direction to fulfillment. We are in different worlds—although lately that gap has been delightfully shrinking—and while I glimpse her thoughts, she doesn't know she also sees, and sometimes feeds, mine. And as I'm surrounded by so many—snickering, vile, hateful, unlike myself, I assure—who'd do anything to finally possess a physical body, I feel myself both excited and somewhat hesitant as my own time approaches.

Much to our advantage, they have this constant habit—oh, these spirits in earthly bodies!—of alternating between light and dark, as if unable to tell the difference, or perhaps not even caring to. They could learn from children, but why, when they could just be made as other versions of themselves? Fitting members of society, by all earthly appearances, until they gradually tap into other, more mysterious and macabre activities. At times I'm fascinated, and at others, repulsed by their cluelessness. What is so unclear? It's right in front of them! And *created in His image*, so the Good Book says—ha! But it's like they're blind, their vision has been closed off. On and off, on and off, that switch of faith, of doubt, until at last they have to finally see for themselves—test it!—and by then their world is turned upside down. Just a little inclination is an invitation, and that's all it takes for one of us to finally get in. So easy: gullible, without concern for protection and, just as surprising to us, unaware they're surrounded by angels—those burning light bearers that repel the dark ones. But I'll somewhat soften my criticism: we usually can't see the angels either unless they allow us, because they're from higher realms. Yes, even on this side we know that He went to their earthly world—the chosen land! Hence, the location all creation is always yearning to enter—and yet even I've been surprised to discover how many there do not believe in it. All the same, it's all to a discarnate entity's benefit.

And while they love to think times haves changed, in many ways they haven't. For although they have in physical ways, the spiritual is both much simpler... and complicated. Same contrasts: whereas in the past, they saw evil everywhere, now they say it doesn't exist—so sure that rational "reasoning" of theirs will keep them safe. And yet who the point of reference? I guess they don't know that each comes with consequences, and feeds my ambivalence about this supposed "blessed" race. Regardless, the natural order will always be, just like we'll never disappear, and we can always find a way. With all their progress, it's ironic to see that they've also regressed—but some will say, it all depends on whom you ask.

So they smile, go on with their lives, so sure what they're doing is right, blameless no matter what. Most convenient are those who have very low, or perhaps even *no* filter—"open to everything," they say with gleaming grins—because that just makes it all easier. That's why some say, those others around me, that this is *our* perfect time, because each era seems to bring them further and further away from light. I don't know why, but something about that feels so wrong, so I keep it to myself, lest I be thought conflicted.

Rose is her name, and how fitting for one as beautiful as ripe for influencing, for each rose has its thorns. Orange-red was her waist-long hair, living in her world of rainbows and velvety-soft, fluffy stuffed toys, bouncy floral dresses and glitter nails, a perpetual smile on her face. Engulfed in that ray-of-sunshine happiness, always eager to help, a cheerful countenance that made her a pleasure to be around, for everyone wants what makes them feel good, and makes them forget their own sufferings. Except for those who want more of it; that is also easily arranged—I know many of the others love to do it. Oh, the gentle Rose, her emerging pliable thorns cultivated by her environment.

Change—and that's where I come in; eager to manifest and assert myself—but so many don't care enough about the consequences to first ask the right questions. Clearly they've forgotten their fairy tales. But even so, many have such warped understanding (although it wasn't always that way), that even when given the answers they simply don't hear them. After all, their children know, always will, but all the same they are (often conveniently to my kind!) dismissed. And so it doesn't take much—only their will—to allow us to navigate into subtle openings. What a marvel that the monster under the bed is very often... right in front of them, but instead of sending it away, they welcome it right in.

Enter a few overbearing, manipulative, deceivingly strong "friends." Easily impressed upon, reeking of dominative neediness—*Accept* me! *Like* me!—fallen prey to what they see via this popular pastime they call "social networking" (and yet, how often isolating, if seeing their true feelings!).

That perfect, boundless place to be what one wishes... so why not engage? Another habit with them: when they try so hard, spend so much time aiming to display on their body what is within—and sometimes it's a true reflection—and often it isn't. The lure for many of my kind is the way that earthly beings can appear one way but truly be another. It's that essence of deception that cannot be maintained for long in our spiritual world, all thanks to that crucial rule of correspondence that Swedenborg was allowed to write copiously about. Yet even he was ridiculed in that 18th century Age of Reason!

It makes many here laugh, and yet it's just all too familiar: that craving for adoration, the world bowing down to your reign—uncontested worship! There, in the domain they call *internet*, this dark, powerful image projected, yielding so many followers. Real fakeness: this idol to venerate in that ephemeral space fed by energy, constantly creating a "reality." The reluctant, sensitive, confused souls thinking they should do the same strange things, take it as inspiration and look up to *them*, as if they themselves aren't worthy enough. But they are, oh if only they knew how much they are, then less of us would succeed in causing harm (and I'm aware I shouldn't technically be revealing that). They could be stronger if they just returned to the Crucified One. Instead, they doubt, feel ashamed for the wrong things and no shame for shameful things, and start doing the same things to prove they also "fit in." Haven't they read that there are many mansions? There is always a place to be in, especially here. So conflicted—so why don't they listen to it? Is that torment not answer enough? But I see how I must not be such a bad soul, for even I have my moments of sympathy for those fragile souls. Perhaps when united, together we'll be something greater than any one of us could've imagined being on our own.

Caged in the material, they've forgotten it's not all there is, for they're always surrounded by spirits. Eager to cross the line, but the price of revelation is knowledge. The height of reasoning: nothing—or the wrong things—sacred, everything's a joke, so somehow try to fill the greedy void. And what better way than her friends who dabble in these "occult" practices, ready to show what veritable powerful witches they are—and I laugh because they don't even know what that means! But it's quite popular these days; to be that mean-vibing sinister girl, long-nailed "earth goddess" who consorts with plants, in her self-made mock-garden of Eden—where it all began. A persona to emulate: tending to the seed, roots growing, quickly spreading, ensnaring; all harmless until they've made it rot, because they want it. After all, they do have free will.

People to Kill, reads the caption on the black faux leather gothic purse. Isn't it funny, that overt display of humor—and on a product full of toxic ingredients. And what if it was an outright confession? (And more interestingly: what would they *do* about it?) *Down with my demons, Made by Satan*; the letters creep upon the surface of t-shirts—fashion, identification, sarcasm, perhaps a conglomeration? Loving (worshipping?) animals; vegan and earth friendly, yet adorned in clothes made by emaciated employees in obscure factories. Oh, the laughable irony of their ignorance, except, of course, when it isn't. For in their very real world, many do not see past their own wishes, which is simply to adorn their physical selves, and sacrifice whatever lofty ideals they claim to have, ethics be damned.

Oh, if only they knew that it'll be just as they wished... although of course perhaps not exactly as expected. But that's the thing with life, isn't it? *It's full of surprises*; that's what they say when they can no longer control it. But if they only looked deeper at their naked intent, they might be more honest on the real source of their goals, and it would be clearer how it may unfold. No mere surprise at all! But then again, true that He also does intervene all too often—the ultimate frequency barrier, so keen on protecting His creation—who so often rejects Him. But that's just another opportunity, as many here love to fuel their misunderstandings, their conviction that they're *alone*. Nevertheless: saving the children, over and over, until the end of time. Sometimes I'd like to see Him lose his patience with them, but after all this time I doubt it'll ever happen.

The glimmer in her Rose-eyes shifts, replaced by some kind of melancholy and sadness. *This horrible world we live in*—her poetic, feeling soul senses, sympathizes with it and I know she's hovering between the worlds because it's all too full of love and caring for her neighbor, and so I have to work with that. What works is when gradually her fiendish friends, selfish, rebellious, want revenge. On what, whom? It's enough that the intent is there! Hence the opportune way to slither in, because now they've started thinking themselves the lawmakers and righteous sources of justice. Yes; these proud girls, thinking it's all their own power, unaware that another (if not more!) has slipped in, and indulged their cruel fancies—and at the core they know they wanted it that way. And then there's Rose, my tentatively prickly Rose enrobed in her trepidation and questioning sense of self.

She was never into those "magic" symbols now emerging everywhere, especially pentagrams. For all her doubting, she is quite smart—perhaps that's why I've chosen her—for she knows the symbols themselves don't have meaning: it's all in the use of it and power given it. But imagine the potential fun for me when they don't truly know—or admit—the true intent, so long as they have their glory and can appear wise in their special, secret ways. So once more, following the pattern, her friends lead the way: posing in front of mirrors and windows with burning candles, at cemeteries and (usually fake) castle ruins, on misty or rainy days, and here she is, brooding and stamped with that symbol on her chest. But at least she's sexy, no? She has the look of being into bondage, and why wouldn't she want to give that impression when it's what will get virtual attention?

And when her Rosey conscience is troubled, trying to justify: *I just like how it looks, it doesn't mean anything.* But then why wear it? And why wear that symbol and not others, which might offend even more people? (The swastika: I *know* you're thinking it!) So then her sensitivities are there, but she's selected some and left the others! And can something which has an effect on her—positive or negative—be so benign? Oh, how they love to pretend they don't know when they do!

She's a writer and her verses that once spoke of light and heavenly love are now overcome by cheerless, dreary heaviness. Her struggle: should it be to expose that darkness and warn the world, or to wallow in its filth, maybe even secretly wish others to feel it? For surely they are not the same things, and I'm there when she's reflecting on her frustration. She feels quite strongly—more than others, including those who call themselves her friends— and she's rocking in her corner, crying as she struggles with that rising sense of dread of something terribly wrong but unsure how, or even if, to speak out against it, to go her own way. Dare she say it: to walk the path alone, if that be the requirement. And I don't think she knows that it's at those moments when she's strongest, and I'm torn, transfixed, wanting to tell her that.

Sometimes she draws, alternating her doodles of menacing disfigured forms. Then the books on magic and conjuring spirits that her friends tell her to read, claiming they've already started seeing results and she should try it. But one thing catches her eye: automatic writing. What is it? Would it help enhance her skill and the process? Just imagine: it'll be easier to finally *automatically write*! She reads the stories, curious and fascinated about people who say they've felt energies overcome them, and it's as if the hand moves by itself, writing things whose content they don't know until they later read the text! A peculiar experience: sensing that force course through and then leave, and some have repeated it many times. The thought grows in her mind—for that's where it all starts—and she sets the day when she'll finally take the plunge. She can't know how it'll go: just sit and call on something, and see what happens; a feeling I somewhat echo.

That day, Rose sits at her candle-lit table, looking as pale as the blank paper. Pen in hand, she keeps her eyes closed while her thoughts repeatedly ask: *Whoever wants to say something come through, whoever wants to say something come through*. Her hand glides across the page, anticipating—but nothing happens because I wait. Will I actually do this?

A few minutes pass and her thoughts trail off to nothing specific—her guard lowering—as gradually she floats elsewhere, growing sleepier by the second. Here's my chance at last and yet there I am, hesitant. But the widening tunnel beckons and finally I slip in, slowly, and her right arm is mine by way of the back of her head, winding down and around that long, narrow space in time. She feels a heaviness, then her arm going numb, and she's in a trance as I make her write, easy things to test it out.

Hi, it's me.

She tenses, even as I feel a smile creep on her lips at the confirmation: *it's really working!* But her resistance goes up—both happy and shocked—that she starts to shake, retreating, so that without intending to she blocks the flow, and that's all that happens that time. She takes her time before finally looking at the evidence, almost in denial of what happened. *Me?* Who is *me?* And once more she drifts in that familiar space between wanting to know and never asking again.

Rose tells her friends of this first instance, and they coax her on, although secretly jealous that she should have such immediate results; she who's sub-par, not even a real, well, anything really; basically "behind in everything" compared to them. She ponders over what to do, as if she should do anything differently the next time, and I myself wonder what I'll tell her.

And then it dawns on me: it just might be the time to cross over and take over for good: no more waiting or going back.

The promised day comes, and as before I drift into the widening passage, take over her arm and animate her fingers as she feels herself again writing, her eyes pinched shut with concentration. Resolved to the curious sensation, this time she's more permitting, part of her withdrawing for me to fill the space, as I immerse myself ever more so into her. There's only so much surface, I find, in this physical body, and I don't know why it somewhat disappoints me. I become more aware of the layers of it all, and how hard it must be for them to feel trapped as they struggle to escape the places they often claim not to want to be in.

Suddenly I feel a pulling, overbearing strain and I know it's not my doing, and even less hers. I fight it, asserting myself, and it's then that we hear a gritty, raspy echo: *I'll fight you for it; she's mine! I'll step in and give her that; fill the void she's made, isn't that what she wanted? Seeking to be someone else; well then the outcome can hardly be so surprising!*

For a moment Rose freezes, even as she feels her heart pounding ever faster, harder in her throat. Regret engulfs her: her eyes fly open, gasping as she shakes, because she's then become truly afraid. Her wrist rattles, fist locked around the pen, transcribing the message fast as lightning. She lets out a muffled cry as her arm quickly goes from tingling, to warm, to burning, as I stand my ground, covering her with my own commanding energy.

Minutes stretch, and at last I've forced the other away, and I take a moment to make sure it's clear before I make my own retreat. Panting, she wipes her brow, repeating over and over, *It's ok, it's over, it's ok.* I wonder which of the others had the nerve to try to claim my designated being, and it's then that I realize: I defended her on impulse. A strange, although not unpleasant feeling overcomes me, and though I can't quite say, it's unlike anything I've ever felt.

She never really settles as much as she wants, her innermost being rattled, already fearing that she'll never be the same, but at last musters the courage to read the note: *Don't do it again.*

Though deep down I detect a hint of smiling, relieved agreement, restlessness overcomes her as she ponders: what happened? But most importantly, *why* did she do it? For what purpose? What was she missing? She digs deeper, finds the alarming accounts of paralysis, increasingly hard to shake off whatever that *thing* is, because all they know is that it's not their doing, and the truth sets in: they've invited *something else* in. And I know for I've seen it happen so many times myself, though I've never been the one to infiltrate. The misunderstanding of the whole affair sets in, as she realizes it wasn't as she'd hoped, and it certainly wasn't about her enriching her own writing skill; rather it's another entity getting what they want at the cost of her own will.

And I can't help but rejoice when I see that resolve come over my Rose, her timely intelligence peeking through: it's easier to prevent something than try to remove it once it's already in. A sense of pride at my achievement fills me—for without me she might've not come to that conclusion—proving that she heard me after all. If she didn't before, now she knows that she only has to seek and trust the Holy Ghost without needing to mess with these unknown, potentially harmful things, and I know because I could've been one of them.

It always comes back to the same thing: the mind and its influences, whose control is only possible because of Him. Growth only comes with improving, and we both have. But I can't deny my own role in it: I thought I wanted to hurt her, and at a time I did. But now I want to help, and even though it was all so fast, I know now that it can be that way when you're reset in your new direction. And yet, already I hear my own doubt protruding: why would it be so simple? If being human is the art of complicating things, then I'm not sure I'm ready for it. Or perhaps I'll just have to be another kind of being, for I've been given a new role and have now become one of her guides, supervised by her angels obeying the highest authority. And though I wanted a body—perhaps always will—I've realized that I don't want to embody her. I want my own, if He allows it, even as we all know that earth is the hardest school of all the planets.

At last, Rose returns to herself—fueling that unique spark within that cannot be duplicated—and adjusts her world and those in it; the sacred garden renewed and blooming after the storm. Her life roughed by the added edge of knowledge, the darkness hovers, but the rainbow is there, which I've now been tasked to help nurture. It's only for a time, as neither of us will be here forever, and my assignment will change as much as hers will.

Still, there's no going back once you know; its remnants driving a life's work henceforth. And though I can now freely and happily say it won't be me, there'll always be others—of varying degrees of destructive filth—prowling, waiting for that smallest opportunity to invade, if only she makes herself receptive.

THREADS OF LIFE

It's the last time, echoes the familiar soft whisper, even as I know all too well that it won't be.

I've said it before: that that was it, just *one more, one last thing*, and then I'd finally have everything I could want, at last—I promise! But it's stronger than me and I respond to beauty, so how could I, a mere human being, resist it? Turn away, but what if it's my duty to yield to it? Not so long ago it was said, as the weaker gender, that it was all I had to care about or even to give. But if I am indeed that simple, then why the struggle? So while it is not all, it is part of it, of me, and even I can't deny that I love it.

I don't remember, don't know how I got here, but then again, does anyone? But there I am, standing, staring, lost in a trance as we're facing each other again, each demanding the other surrenders. The perfect dress: hovering, unearthly in all its striking floral glory—black, laced with red-coral roses, sharp thorny stems entwining, slithering everywhere across the fabric, blurring beginning and end. Dual-tone velvet petals, light, shaded, commanding attention in their elegant restraint. I run my fingers gently against the smooth surface until it leaves its faint yet unmistakable fragrance on my fingertips. And for a moment I wallow in that impression that I am that, and it is me.

If I swore not long ago that I had it all, I am not deceitful if I am now saying the same about this other garment. I could not have lied, when this is different, again, as it always is. For the fact remains that those roses are perfect, and what a miracle that I found the dress, just there, untouched, knowing before I even set eyes on it that it was made for me. But sometimes

I also like that bittersweet torment, that tease: I *do* have everything, and so I leave it, walk away, because beauty will always find me no matter where I am.

And follow me it does, day and night: the gorgeously tormenting fabric now the all-pervading tapestry of my life. I always see them: visions of what could happen when these concepts and lives—in other, eternal dimensions—and I unite, and it's always the same story: *It's a great idea, now how can I materialize it? What will I do about it—follow it? Enough: I must have enough, just in case!* Taking and giving, giving and taking, over and over. Endless breathtaking scenes, whose lengths of immersion vary, and when I leave some I may return to earlier visions at a later time, now evolved, refined since our time apart. That is the cycle of my life. If it's wrong to always see this, and even if I could stop it, I don't know that I would.

Still, I don't need it. But oh, that torturous delight; as if someone is always looking inside my head and now the very thing exists, and I just passed it. Was I wrong, this time? Enough, or never enough? And even if it won't be me, someone else will surely be suited for it. But if the matter is so trivial, there wouldn't be such inner conflict—the constant guilt and justification battling. Why that relentless gnawing, distracting me from other things; that sense of loss lingering? *What have I lost—forever!*

True to the call, I return and she's still there, unblemished, repeating: *Don't you see, I'm made for you, and you for me.* Almost instantly, maybe for the first time, I catch myself asking: who *is* that talking? Is it my positive thoughts, my ego? Is it something else? And how to distinguish them? But this time, a peaceful enthusiasm overcomes me—oh, the marvels of unexpected combinations! Perfect, now even on sale, the decision is made and like that she's mine. It may be said that we always make excuses for our desires, but if anyone has lived without ever, at any time, yielding to theirs, I'd like to talk to them.

There's always that anticipation to the first wear, like finally meeting another long lost part of myself. Butterflies in the stomach: *Where have you been all this time?!* No matter, for here we are at last reunited. And I want to say it's everything I imagined, but that's not quite it, because it's so much more, casting my senses into chaos. And now I'm not sure what it all is, except that this new thing, new self—and yet how *familiar* it is!—is there, and I love it. How long has it been, since I was last that person? So primal, delightfully ancient; like returning to the undiluted source of it all.

A vision, at once clamoring to the world, and yet reluctant to so easily reveal it. The constant question of whether to share or preserve: *unworthy, it's too much, it'll be misunderstood, someone will take offense, better change it*—something, always something. But who am I living for and why should I have to explain? And life goes on: a series of things, big and small, I wanted to accomplish but didn't simply because of fear of endless outside commentary. Like people have nothing else to do—and maybe they don't—and what does that have to do with me? A clear recipe for misery I've long flushed down the sad drain.

It takes me a few moments to realize that I'm dancing in this lovely second skin, because that's how transported I am. How happy *it* makes me, or is that *me* being happy in it? Oh, so different, this feeling, even as I try to convince myself I already know it. This happiness—the very reason I want more of it. The ironic beauty of feeling more myself in some other piece, in someone else's clothing—or *did I* create it, when it found me, and I now own it!—for I am unmistakably filled. A suffocating joy, my heart pounding—and I almost want to cry. Cry! That is how I know it's *new* and *real*, defies mere human description: the emotion surfacing from some concealed place because I've never reacted that way, no matter how nice all the pieces in my collection have been. The intensity surges through me: a longing for another, better life to be lived, so close yet out of reach somehow, even as people of all kinds pass me by every day, but we might as well be on different planets—and maybe we are. Just floating spirits, claws out and ready to strike whoever comes too close, and that's the armor ever in action, doing its job. And though I'm fine with it, it's also nice to know that I don't need it, that I can also remove it sometimes, maybe even more often than that.

The lovely garment is well housed in a part of the closet, but often she's just out, reclining about, for my hungry eyes to feast on. The conundrum: shall I stop, give her a break—maybe eat some actual food whose taste I'm almost forgetting? But isn't that diminishing by doubting her supernatural strength? Mostly, when I feel it I don't need to rationalize: just go with it, and like that I'm wearing the dress a lot more than I usually would, or have done with any other. *An occasion*—the way to justify it. *What* occasion?

I'm alive and that's enough! Alive and happy, so here we are, and I don't know or care what time or day of the week it is; that I should have to explain it carries its own sadness.

Something always happens. Surely that's why I went along with it, constantly refueling my excitement; that proud, satisfied conviction that it's unlike anything else that came before. For a time I dismiss it, but it's there. I look for other words, but it comes back to the same: I *hate* it—it makes no sense! Because how can I have that repulsive feeling then, when I'm wearing it, of all times? When the garment is—dare I say it—possibly the one truly perfect dress I own? Like I may finally have reached that elusive point! And then, again, the oddest thought: she's trying to tell me something! And it's my job to go with it, when that's exactly what I did by hearing her call and bringing her into my life.

When you're in love, you look at things differently; the overflowing, pure, undiluted fire deepening your sense of sight. So I stare: eyeballs darting, burying, lost in the endless sewn patterns as I count the threads, always losing my place. Thirty in half an inch? No, more than that. A labyrinth of paths, destinations unknown, frustrating for lack of answers; no ending, no future. Enough or never enough! Where was this going? Over and over, frantically, determined bony fingers flickering faster and faster; needle digging, burying, in and out, in and out—and I flinch, my fingers seeking instant refuge in my mouth. That undeniable taste of iron I like. Blood on my fingers... and I didn't even notice it. But worst of all, that ache, oh that ache in my joints! Thin ligaments barely held together; so sure my fingers will fall off—maybe I'll even cut them off, if only it'll lessen the pain! A ghostly whip strikes me at this: how dare I even *think* such a thing: these hands, eyes—the whole body!—are a *gift*, and that's something we all too easily forget! So on it goes: a deep pride and satisfaction resurfacing, filling me up, reminding me that this pain is at least proof of my labored existence.

I hear my deep breathing and realize I'm panting—with no thought tht for how long it's been. I would laugh but it still feels too disturbing. What is this habit that I sometimes have: let myself get sucked into a crazy idea and be drawn into it... Seconds, only seconds it takes to look real, and sometimes every cell in my body reflects belief in the vision. That's all it takes, and there's as much a beauty as a deeply concerning aspect to this. Why, why, why? Too sensitive, creative, imaginary, tired; all quick explanations to dismiss it.

There's an irony to a love that by turns fills me with such endless energy, then leaves me feeling drained. That amazing power that demands everything, makes me forget all else, among them my basic needs, because all I care about is wearing it, and just walking, and going, and walking and going some more. High, my brain buzzing, aware I haven't closed my eyes in days and all the lights around me are too bright, even the dim ones, and still my eyeballs stare, bulge out of their sockets, nearly ready to pop out. Catching every moment, staying on task: must get this detail, this stitch, right—enough or not?—consistently, and then I'll be done and I'll finally be able to go home and sleep. But it doesn't end and I'm concerned because for the first time I'm thinking: this might be hell. But I must not ungratefully think that way.

Always on the go: worrying about, and sometimes catching some train, in a hurry, restless. And I *hate* that feeling too; it's part of what I hate the most in life. I've never been like this—and I instantly stop, catch myself knowing that's a lie, only it was so long ago. But even after all this time I know the reality of the pain too well, that phantom constantly creeping over our earthly flesh, making sure we don't forget. But I take comfort in thinking that at least it's while wearing my favorite piece. We are in this together, and I am her faithful passenger.

It calms and I'm happy again; how could I ever have doubted her? Out again, immaculate, and I'm walking on clouds at the lovely sunny park. Moist emerald grass kisses my feet and my head spins as I turn and turn in the heavenly lush garden, until I collapse and still I spin as my heavy eyelids close. There's a roar somewhere, and it all shakes, unstoppable waves of vibrations bursting as everything crumbles around me. We look at each other for answers—how to stop it?—but we're all frozen in that unstable, frightening place, different levels of fear and confusion smeared on our faces. I see red: concrete blocks smashing onto fabrics, undyed, simple and meticulously embroidered alike, all subjected to the same fate. All the time it took, now to start it all over again! But how could I: my flesh pounded, crushed with unbearable weight, suffocating, lungs on fire as I try to breathe, take short painful breaths. Slow, everything is so slow now—and that strange, almost cruel calmness, of all things!—and I reach, still trying to hurry!—but where to? And I become aware that now things will never be the same.

Something must've changed, disconnected, and I pause, because looking down below at my earthly form I almost don't recognize myself. Cheekbones caved in, emaciated limbs, and that's when I realize I haven't eaten enough in a while. Appetite gone, but I have reasons: lack of resources, and so I constantly choose the same: just work and sew, and make, make, make and then I'll finally have enough—of money, of health, of clothes, of love—of everything! It hurts, every limb battered, and the only thing that keeps me going is clinging to that hope, that wish that I'm just inches, maybe even millimeters, away from the right door that will finally open and change everything. A new beginning, and somehow all this sadness and emptiness would have been worth it, if I could just *reach it*—but in that moment I can't help but think that somehow I failed, and it's too late.

Time vanishes, because I have no idea when I'm brought to my senses, and the man at my side stares at me with a mix of relief and concern. A nightmare: that's what it feels like, but so vivid! I reassure him—he is ready to accompany me home, a kind soul—but I do it as much for him as for myself. My arms hug my torso, and though I've indeed shed weight, I'm also not as bad as I imagined—*saw*—the grotesque lingering feeling of darkness sending shudders down my spine. I'm on my feet and eyes linger on me, I know, because that's what the dress does, and always will, provoke: admiration, awe of perfection—her constant expanding beauty proof of her supernatural endurance.

By the time I get home I feel a bit better, thankful for my ever-welcoming haven, just as I left it: loaves of untouched bread, ripe fruits in the basket, desk, papers, and bookcases, trinkets, the colorful closet—the spaces we make for love, where everything somehow always comes full circle.

I'm still in the dress when I finally sit, grab the nearest newspaper, and for a moment my chest tightens just as it did a short while ago at the park. A clothing factory, collapsed building, workers dead... but miraculously, some survivors. Caught between terror and relief—even the thought of opening my own shop someday. A familiar tearful portrait and instantly I *know* who she is: her soul, her feelings, her whole life, because I saw them all, and lived them all myself, long ago. A love permeating our achievements, knitting endlessly with care, exhaustion be damned, calling to me, grazing my skin all the way down to the raw, scraped bones. Some will say it's trivial to be this meticulous, but they must not know that it makes all the difference, even if it takes longer than you thought to reach its desired form. You just work, and work some more until you know it's done, and finally, slowly, release it to its own journey, as you continue your own.

It alternates between easy and hard, but the work is its own reward. The passages open, connecting us, and we'll always find and uplift each other, in one form or another, because that's what true love does. And for the first time, to know that this endless cycle never ends is comforting.

RESIDENCE

I.

It's said criminals often like to come back to the scene of their crimes—and what satisfying rush for me to be tasked to track them down. I like returning to certain locations, like a wandering gypsy traveler with no fixed abode. Ever on a holy mission, I've no fear of being seen, not when the world is so busy, busy, busy with endless *more important* things. That's perfect when I not only like, but need my peaceful quiet.

For me it's the Holy Land, Italy, Germany, France, Spain, California, and especially Brussels. But let's be honest: the list will likely keep growing.

I once thought that having a physical threat would be easier for people to deal with; somehow more reassuring in that at least they can identify it and monitor it, in a sense—maybe even defeat it. But I know better now, because the heart of man is to be indifferent no matter the circumstances.

Take pandemics, on which everyone's become an expert. Asymptomatic; so it's not a problem until it is, at which point it's become a problem with clear physical signs. But even with that logic, in the chaotic fray, the unsettling allure of the unknown remains: that invisible force that we all know, in endless diluted ways, even though many will pretend it doesn't exist, or only does in the way they imagine it. Everyone has it, but some will say it's the heart of artists to work with and in that, yielding a shifting tunnel path of light and dark.

Dangerous or safe? To go or not go? Do the facts add up, can they be trusted enough to guide the next steps? But it doesn't matter who says what, because in the end people do what they want anyways. Certainty and doubt, and for some the achievement is in that constant vacillation, refusal to choose, to create and name, as if that kept them "open-minded," and therefore safe. Yet God gave Adam dominion over the animals in the Garden of Eden.

That's where artist-writer residence programs come in, to push those inclined out of their shells and empty themselves—and part of their wallet, too. Here the material price can play its part in considering your worth, because nothing is more satisfyingly torturous to creators than comparing themselves to *others*. So why not do it for a good price? At least you'll be in a breathtaking, richly imposing historical setting with uninterrupted time and endless creative inspiration, because it doesn't exist anywhere else but in *that residence*. Somewhere deep in your subconscious you know it could've been anywhere, but in the end, that's where you end up.

Of course, *en France* again. There's so much packed there, as there is anywhere, and it keeps calling and saying I should tell about it—whenever and whatever it is that will manifest and clarify itself to me. So then, perfect time to return and do some writing, albeit this time in a restored 18th century château. And until the subject is decided, I'll enjoy other things, too; like painting, poetry, or even hunting. You can never fully know how the inspiration will hit or what it will bring. But over time the once subtle feeling, that sense of being called, grows stronger, so like an eternal, unrestricted ghost, I'm on constant pilgrimage.

Alsace is perfect, historically taking turns being French or German, maybe both when convenient. So I pack two big suitcases, one for clothing and a significant health kit, and the other for tools of the trades.

Then, one gloriously foggy fall afternoon, I arrive to the 18th century red-bricked castle sequestered among an army of giant shadowy firs. The fiery light invitingly shines through the gaping French windows, a delicious pervading scent hinting at nearby fresh baguettes. Welcomed and guided by a friendly hostess, on my way up I glimpse the long dinner table covered in cold cuts and silverware, glistening like the raging fireplace. Just as I hoped, it's a mix of elegance and rustic charm, neither too soft or hard.

My room is on the top floor, past lovely intricately carved stairs, entirely silent just the way I love it. It's much bigger than the *chambre de bonne* I'd lived in in Paris before, and if it had been one before, the expansion is such that it's nearly impossible to tell. In any case, having space in a European country is always a welcomed gift, and if it's the Wild West Californian inclination for space, I make no apologies for it. With some friendly cautious exchanges, it doesn't take long for me to find that I'm to be the only one on that floor—they're able to accommodate my dead serious request for quiet—and I breathe a bit easier for it.

I lay out my Bible next to my bed, and a copy of Gustave Doré's illustration of *Christ coming out of the tomb*, smiling at his glowing form looking at me. And like any true creative, I unsurprisingly leave the rest packed: the faithful tools are incubating and will come out soon enough. No need to pretend that I'll get started on stuff right away; not when I'm taking in the gorgeous veil of fog wrapping around the valley of sensible fir trees.

Evening orientation is announced so I drift slowly along the long, dark hall echoing with old and new energy, and back down to the low pulsating hubbub of the gathering. Like most civilized introductions, everything is pleasantly calculated: glowing faces excited to have landed in this special place that will surely transform all the raging life that's long been brewing within.

We're a tribe of like minds! We understand each other!—Our longing, searching souls whisper, because we all had that same wild idea to make the journey just to arrive there and take *this thing* seriously, in all its meanings.

There are six of us as visiting creatives, totaling three men and three women, and I joke that the Seventh is of course our inner Muse, united in dwelling on the Other Side until they finally come through each of us. Heads nod as one: it's a dream for us to be there and come together in this strangely exciting time. And as laughter echoes over our communal lacking of the media's agreed-upon symptoms of the sickness, it's reassuring to think that if anyone gets sick, the host is naturally prepared for that, too. Anything less would be downright murderous, though none of us can pretend not to know at least some of the risks involved.

It turns out that every other visitor is a painter but me, or at least, does it professionally. I've painted all my life but it makes me realize for the first time that I've done it for love without thought—or is it want?—of monetizing it. In these uncertain and changing times, maybe I should start considering it, but just the next concern of how to go about pricing and judging its value makes me gladly abandon the thought for the time being.

What are you going to write?

The dreaded lurking question comes at last, and I say that I don't know; that I love history and the way it influences, and even merges with our present, and surely there's something that will come through, maybe even involve us as a group. The fear of disappointment makes me nearly regret saying it, but that's what came to mind—plus I hardly expect anyone to remember, when I know how easily people forget, especially when it's not about themselves.

We talk of potential picnics, fishing and cruising on the Rhine River, and trips to Strasbourg, Colmar, and other nearby cities, but no word on hunting so I don't mention it, or maybe I'll ask the host later. As the arrival day, everyone is jet-lagged, so though it's a pleasant wine-filled evening around the living room fireplace, it's an early night in. We trickle off and up the stairs to our rooms, and I happily float to mine on the topmost floor.

It's a small safe town where many keep their doors unlocked—the host and his staff repeated—but I lock my door and silently lean a chair against it without a second thought. Others can do as they please, and so will I. I've always loved the deep silence for allowing me to better hear, and the requisite lack of internet is another lifted burden of distractions, too.

I go to my tools of the trades suitcase and, barely opening it, I reach into it and blindly pat, confirming that what I packed is still within. Satisfied, I change into some comfy PJs, turn out the lights and go to the windows to draw the thick curtains shut.

I'm at the last window when a swift, sweeping movement down below catches my eye, and by instinct I retreat to the side to peek safely out of sight. Stomach clenched I wait, complete silence permeating like the constant, now almost eerie mist. I'm thinking I need sleep and should just get on with it—until I catch it again, a dark shadow now further away at left, as if it'd moved off in the opposite direction.

That's it: no need to imagine what's there. Some curious lurker, wanting to see the new residents.

Late at night. In the pitch dark.

And you wonder why I'm always prepared.

II.

The night is a blur, but I awake refreshed to the echo of some metal clinking and faraway, sporadic squawking. We breakfast on omelettes, croissants, fruits, tea and coffee, and decide to begin our first full day with a hike nearby. We head east towards the creek, the grounds and air moist with the autumn mist. There aren't many neighbors around, and the few we see are friendly and welcoming.

The gushing surroundings yield flushed elation, the happy spark for endless painted scenes. Our chats lead me to ask if they believe that any subject is off limits for painting, and would they ever self-censor? The answer is generally no; that it's the realm of art to explore, although what gets explored is naturally based on any creator's interests. So here I bring up the concern not to offend.

Well, better not do anything ever, then, chuckles one of them.

But some will criticize, maybe even project their hate on your misinterpreted work—I push, surprised that the conversation is going the way I hoped.

Maybe, but we all have enough self-hate on our own without needing to add another's, and creating is how we seek to make things better, no matter how much we still fail, no?

The answer is great, of course, but even then I can't deny what I hear; the tremor lurking, that allure to please and look a certain way, appearing oh-so-defiant. In short, saying what we all want to hear. But time tests us all.

Like art itself, we come back to this concept of abstract, and how we can only scratch the surface, and though I've yet to see their works, several refer to their work as abstract and others as landscape artists.

We return for an early afternoon lunch and then drift to our spaces to reconvene with our first day's discoveries. I go to my room, but I don't feel like writing, not with that gnawing feeling that there's more exploring needed, more answers to be sought. I go to my tools of the trades suitcase, shuffle through it and bring out the bundle smelling of heavenly rose-scented incense. I unroll it, exposing my hand gun, and slip it into my padded coat's large inside pocket, and with a sigh of satisfied relief, venture out on my own again.

I head northwest into the trees this time, along where I saw the previous night's receding shadow. Nothing unusual, that I can see—but sight is often the most misleading sense. I've known this all my life, just like I've known I would own and carry firearms, at the very least. Oh France and its laws, and I could obviously care less, when its government hardly changes in the face of threats. But I know how to handle them, and this should be no exception. Except, I have no way to prove it; to show that this tormenting nagging is real, that something is going to happen, and is part of the reason why I've come.

Thankfully the forest has its soothing way of restoring my breath. Our own God came to earth and was hung up on a tree-cross, though many forget and some don't care at all. But my anguish is such that sometimes I selfishly, vainly think maybe it is enough, for me to feel all this to make up for those who don't; like I might put in a word for them.

It's not something I have to make myself do; it just happens that before I know it I'm deep into the woods, feeling better, unafraid, one with the elements. Sitting amongst the trees, just listening to the sounds of life that He created—even the evil in it, though at that moment it's so far away. Humbled, I'm filled with gratitude that He'll always put me right where He wants me, no matter my limited understanding or unworthiness for the task.

For a suspended moment of two days, time is idyllic, which is exactly what's needed to pretend that you're fine, safe to be yourself and just create in your own paradise. In those moments you can tell yourself that it was just your mind playing mean, distracting tricks. That's the work of a creative: you imagine, maybe even exaggerate what isn't there. But then why *is it*? The answer is in its presence—asymptomatic until *not!*

Then the dreams—though some call them nightmares—go further: the shadowy figure coming closer. Not just one, but several. Multiple times I awake in a sweat and I *know* what I have to do, but dread the execution. How am I going to tell them? But as with many things in life it's more important to share the message than to worry about its reception.

There's no good time for this conversation, so the third morning I'm just out with it while gathered at breakfast: we are being watched by bloodthirsty entities. It's all been planned and we're about to be attacked. No, it's not a sick joke as material for my writing project, when not only is it not my type but I'd rather not even talk about my work until it's finally, miraculously done, and which—by the shocking way!—I haven't even started on.

But maybe that's my way of kicking it off, and I did mention that I might write about all of us.

Yes, but I'm not saying that this is connected! I'm just worried out of my mind about our safety, and wanting to know what we're going to do now to actually ensure it!

What's this really all about?

I don't know if I'm more surprised or disgusted by the genuine ignorant stares, as if it hasn't been obvious for years that the threat has been lurking. And the worst of it is that it's not just here, but *everywhere*.

You've forgotten the facts, so I'll remind you—I say with a needed shift in tone to clarify that I'm not in the least playing. The château is well-known, and obviously not just locally—its reputation for fostering art, even as it's clearly not able—or is it willing?—to accommodate everyone. Not that it should, mind you, but that makes some even more disgruntled than they already are. Non-inclusive, they'll say, and to me there are bigger priorities than that, but it's just one of many excuses for unhappy types to latch onto.

And that's only one aspect. Stabbings, shootings, drive-ins, decapitations over sketches that others disagree with—that I myself hesitate to call "art"—but is still arguably part of creative expression, no matter our variously similar definitions of it. Combine that with a rolling roster of visitors, in the heart of the countryside, secluded, thinking themselves removed from those pesky city concerns. Unlocked doors, limited communication: do I really need to lay out the obvious benefits for anyone intending harm!

But the frowning stares and crossed arms seem more upset at this inconvenient, uncomfortable sharing of facts than the stark truth that it can not only so easily happen, but is on its way to us as we speak, with only a few days left at best!

I must be exhausted; they know the draining torments of creative energy, and forgive my bout of misled exaggeration. A good night's rest will help.

As if I hadn't tried that approach already, oh so long ago.

But also, it's added, *if it takes a few days, since such things can't exactly be planned, perhaps it's best I keep to myself so that I don't hinder others' creative progress.*

Dismayed, I was going to leave it at that, but I couldn't resist adding to please be careful when they're out and about, and find ways to protect themselves, then left them to work through their confusion.

Though I wish it were under different circumstances, I love this extent of personal space. But with that level of denial I'm even more thankful that I haven't said a thing about my other guns and two AK-47s I brought along. They would think I'm the crazy one, intending harm when I'm only looking to deflect it and always try to stay a step ahead.

In my room I sit in the dark, faithfully glancing at my Bible. Then, when moved by the Holy Ghost, I slowly creep to the window. I wait, motionless, merging with the curtains—then, finally, I see them. They are getting bolder, but only because it's allowed, even welcomed. Why is that so hard to see?

I retreat, and with my arms open I fall back on my bed, the stillness lovingly wrapping me up as it's done for lifetimes.

III.

The distance helps, because the mask was going to come down anyway. The initial days are transitional, to prove to yourself and others that you're normal, but maybe also a bit special—even talented, hence your acceptance and worthiness of being there with them. Or were we just the only gullible, selfish, irresponsible applicants in such an uncertain time, and with the host in need of income like anyone else, who was he to turn us down? Come to think of it, we've seen him the least of all so far.

I said mask, but no need to downplay it, when we have multiple. Work, family, friends, lovers; we like to think we're the same with all of them, but how could we be, when the dynamics vary. They could each paint similar, connected images, or clashing ones. But anyway isn't this the place we came to specifically to tap into them? Why limit yourself! Maybe don't even try to count them—that, at least, removes some stress.

So which one am I now?

I'm an eighth century hooded Bavarian monk, grateful to our Lord for sending Charlemagne—that grandson of Charles Martel—to conquer our region and fight the Saracens in Iberia. I sit cross legged, the raging rose-scented incense swirling wildly all over the room and straight into my nostrils, blessing my brain. Just like the good ol' Holy Land days, casting off *jinn* with my early Christian, desert-dwelling kin and brothers in the faith. I might also be a Sister in Hildegard of Bingen's Rupertsberg monastery which, like her Disibodenberg residence, is located nearby. Surely it's no coincidence that she was born right around the First Crusade.

O Ierusalem, aurea civitas—the glorious chanted lyrics of her poem dance like heavenly doves in my soul. She made drawings too, of her own visions that began when she was only three years old, back in 12th century Böckelheim. Now *there* is a soul who was born refusing to separate her spiritual life from her art, for anything else is incomplete or a lie. Then there's Clemens Brentano, toying with folk tales of the Brothers Grimm, then gravitating to Anne Catherine Emmerich's holy struggle and visions.

I keep praying, envisioning the perimeters of our current dwelling, filling it with protective holy spirits, because that's what exorcists do. I was one then, and I'm one now: these characteristics don't leave so easily. Though I like the vocation enough, it won't be the last time that I feel like a person watching a scenario repeat itself across time. I'm not Catholic or Protestant, or maybe I'm both, and sometimes a bit Eastern Orthodox too, or even Miaphysite, depending on how far back I go.

And to think I could've just stayed where I was... but the story would've been different. That's not a pro or con, just a factual statement. I decided to come, so there's no fussing and regretting: only moving forward.

I'm rocking back and forth in my trance, as I always do while praying, and I realize what that might look like if anyone found me in this state. They'd say I was casting spells, a kind of witch, and then they'd have to retract their doubt, apologize and gather around me, begging for all the details because these days everyone praises witches. But when you say you're Christian praying, that's not exciting, or might even be criminal, so I'm the one some would try to burn at their stake. But I've already done it, and the sad thing is, the tired cycle sometimes repeats because of people's own actions.

Exorcist, not psychic, and you sure don't need me to tell you that even they can't see and hear everything. No one is meant to: that's the most difficult thing for us to hear when we want all the powers all the time. Still we try to do it, typical sad humans, and artists too, but it's dangerous and I keep trying to warn people—but no; *I'm* the one who's the threat! Well they don't have to listen to me, but in His time every knee will bow. They may also listen to whoever else He decides to send along, because the thing is people do listen, but often only to who they want, or if it fits their fragile self-made bubble.

I stick to things that work, and I know it works because every time I come out of my trance—though I try not to, in a way—I feel better. Stronger, ready to take on anything. In His mercy I've glimpsed into His creation, of which I'm not only surprisingly a part, but have a role in.

Strapped as usual, I go out on my fourth early morning walk, guided by the perfect biblical pillar of cloud, while the other residents seem vanished. Hopefully at least they're finally getting work done, as I am, though as usual it's not quite what I expected. But that's part of following orders.

On my walk, I run into a neighbor, an older woman who gives a hesitant but pleasant smile, and I nod back the same and go on, not wanting to disturb her cautious guard. Then she draws near, and after confirming that I speak her language, she seems relieved and asks how things are going over at the château. It's hard to say, I chuckle, but she accosted me, so there must be a reason. I put my best serious face on and add that I hope she, and the whole town, is safe because I don't trust what's coming, or rather, has already long been lurking.

She fixes me, her perceptive eyes sparkling, and through her barely discernible muscle spasm at her temple, I know she understands. Naturally: she lives in it, too! I know then, as I often do, that she and others have been keeping their distance because that's what it is: a chasm between their lives and those who just come for a fun, temporary escape, a mere moment they'll then self-righteously affix in their memories and say reflects the entire truth. Not that it's what everyone does, but the certainty envelops me like a blanket at my realization that this group is particularly susceptible to pampered ignorance.

I eat alone in the evening, like I've done ever since our fall out, and for the first time I fall asleep and awaken on the fifth day with a sense of reassurance. I always feel good when I recall my dreams, and I smile as I see the lingering local General Claudius Drusus in his Roman armor, saying, *They will take care of this.* That's what Roman generals do, with their no-nonsense approach! On that thought, he must approve of nearby Drusenheim being named after him on the site of his former castle. I may not entirely know what it means, but at least it adds to the sense of not being alone, which is what ultimately we're always searching for.

I go down to breakfast at my own time, hoping not to see anyone as has been the pattern, but everyone is silent around the table, timidly eyeing me. Strange, but I fill my plate and am about to leave when I'm addressed by one of the women.

All of us, except one, have had odd dreams. One won't even come out of his room before getting answers from you.

From me? Am I to be believed now? I've said what I had to say: it's not safe and we need to prepare and defend ourselves.

He thinks—he's ready to leave. Do you agree with this? No offense but since you're the one who first mentioned it, why are you still here then?

Because I haven't been assigned to leave. But I will eventually, like everyone else, in due time.

It occurs to me that I might be the only one there who isn't scared. Concerned, definitely; must be the inner exorcist. But scared? That's not the right word, or perhaps it's more like disturbed, even angered, by the sight of traits like indifference and cowardice.

If there's something pushing him to leave, then maybe he should, I say.

He swears that this thing, this ghastly Louis XIV ghost, all tattered and monstrously wigged, with ornate lace for hands battered him with his royal cane—shouting at him to leave, blasting him and his unworthiness.

Sounds like Louis XIV, especially with our friend's Protestant background.

But he doesn't practice!

Not good enough for the Sun King who wants him Catholic, I smirk. I don't add that the proud monarch had caused ample strife in this region, too. But as you know—I say—it sounds like that creatively-induced stress that just requires rest to restore his bout of misled exaggeration, I shrug.

I thought the same but actually—it's never been like this before, for either of us.

It's my turn to stare blankly.

Some Roman general, Drusus I think, was thrashing three of us like—like slaves, said we weren't fit to be under his command. He was so imposing and forceful—so real! How could we all dream this?

Why not? It's not unheard of, but we're not here to do dream analysis, are we? I chuckle.

Two of us—the woman paused to gaze at the other—*were also visited by an angry woman from Trier, saying she was falsely accused of witchcraft, and we'll pay for it if we don't listen to her. Did you see her, too?*

No.

We're worried. What if it happens again tonight? How can we work like this?

Then it happens again, I shrug once more. I'm starting to wonder why I'm even still there, listening to this.

What should we do?

I think you already know, but as usual it might be inconvenient. For starters, you have to decide if it was real or not; this "imaginary" thing that crazily has you reacting by being shaken up. For artists, some might say the answer is pretty obvious. And if so, then take some action and defend yourself. What could be more natural than this instinct of self-preservation, I say to their hesitant faces.

Will you be here?

I am, as much as any of us can say "we're here."

Is that the closest they'll come to admitting they need me? Not that I'm saying I can protect them, no matter how much that would flatter my ego to think.

Before disappearing, I glance at the man who hasn't spoken, and I know he's the only other one who hasn't been bothered by these odd disturbances. He might've agreed with me all along, but stayed silent. Unsurprising, if only to fit in—but also, for the benefit of the doubt, perhaps for his own reasons.

IV.

The next sixth day, I smile at the townswoman again on my walk, the raging storm always reigned in during my forays amongst the wise ancient trees, who've seen as much as I have.

I'm admiring the château from afar on my return when I see a she-shadow come my way, running, out of breath.

Where have I been? One of the women and men lie butchered in the field like sheep!

What? Has the host sent for a doctor and the authorities?

He can't be found! Could it be the sickness, though, you think?

Are you being serious? I yell.

Or what about that dancing plague of 1518, we're not far from Strasbourg...

But no one died from it, unlike the popular myths say!

There's absolutely a sickness here, but right now it's not from the elusive pandemic—I miraculously keep to myself.

Oh, we have to placate him! What—what have we done to provoke him? We know it's our fault, so we'll do whatever he wants, if only he stops!

He? Who says it's a he? It's a group of them, and I promise it's not just men, no matter how much you hate the patriarchy.

She frowns at me. *And just where was I?*

Don't blame your indifference on me! And how do I know it's not all of you, when I've been on my own? And why would I warn you about something that I'd intend to do? But I can prove where I was: I was seen and spoken to, as I have been every morning.

She stands back and we keep our distance, which is what it's been from the beginning, really. Controlled, but too late, and with the wrong person.

The three others spill out of the castle's entrance like demons running out of hell. After catching their breath we—now a group of two men and two women—somehow reasonably decide to stay together and search the grounds. We start with the murdered residents whose throats are slashed and bodies stabbed in several places, from criminals who enjoyed inflicting sadistic harm. We cover the corpses, as much to shield from the horror as for deterring potential hungry creatures. They can't make sense of who could've done this, but I know it's the lurkers who came close to the property for the express reason of frightening—and it's working, at least on them. If only they'd listened and paid attention, they would've *seen*—

Then my blood freezes and I realize that they did—watching dumbly from the windows!—but did nothing to stop it.

Better someone else than them—especially them who most shrugged off such attacks; maybe deep down they even wanted it, like a martyr to the artistic cause! So who and how are they to stop it? Let it be an accident! But I'm not repeating their ugly thoughts back to them—these whispering facts that appear as they will—so I go along for the time being.

The host is nowhere to be found and I voice what we all sense but others are reluctant to say: that he's gone for good. So much for protecting and keeping us safe. Come to think of it, both he and the murdered woman were so downplaying of danger, which can be frighteningly close to asking for it.

Without phones or internet to connect us to the outside world—if such is even ideal—we're left with going to the neighbors, which the others are reluctant to do. They want to stay locked in and await the host who's surely gone to get the very help we need.

It's a bleak gathering with hardly any eating and even less talking. With the palpable tension I almost thought we'd spend the night in a room together, but hesitant caution wins, so that we each split to our own rooms. All the better for me, because I'd already decided I'd go to the neighbors at dawn, regardless of their approval.

Immersed in heavenly rose incense I pray, vainly wishing my sight was strong enough to have all the answers all the time. As usual, my guardian angel reassures and emboldens me with the reminder that it's God's wrath people should fear more than evil spirits who are slaves to weak sin.

Then, the *théâtre* begins and though I want to look away, I also want—need!—to watch it.

The terrorizing masked group—one for each!—swarms the woods, creeping close, so fast that in a moment they're at the castle entrance like ghouls. They blast the door down and sweep right up the stairs, right to the doorstep of my fellow residents. The two men and other woman, who'd barely fallen asleep, now awake in horror, while the invaders sniff out their conflicted fear, and gleefully feed it with maddening, chaotic noises and groans, intent on watching it hellishly grow.

What will you do! I want to scream but am grateful that they're pondering it, too.

Alert and angry, the first man arms himself with several palette knives and defiantly waves them at his knife-wielding attacker, who follows their movements like a mad beast. The attacker lunges and slices off a hand, while the bloodied yet emboldened victim plunges a palette knife into his enemy's throat, causing his retreat with a deafening shriek. The second man doesn't wait and pounces on the invader—ready to bury the legs of his easel into each eye socket—but is unable when faced with a cowardly wail and vanishing ghostly figure.

Now, the woman's heart pounds, her life hanging in the balance. For a moment she hates herself for what looks like the worst decision she's ever made, and I almost cry when somehow she concludes it would've happened anyway. She steps to the ghoul and reaches out her hands.

Take them, she says.

The masked face tilts, the emptiness momentarily disrupted by something like feeling.

Take them, or do I have to do it myself? The woman smiles then chuckles at the dumbfounded fool. *Scared? You want me to do it?* she says, reaching for the knife in the immobile intruder's hand. *I'll be the real-life girl without hands, just like in the Brothers Grimm. I deserve it, maybe we all do.* The knife is in her hand then at her wrist. *One, then the other might be with my mouth*—the blade goes slowly into her skin, drawing a red line as a howl erupts then recedes along with its dark source.

I face my door as the darkness approaches, and I myself don't know—am grateful *not* to know!—what will come. But what I do know and don't deserve to is that because of Him no evil ever has the last say. My doorknob rattles and I brace myself, and though I've seen it before in various forms it never becomes easier to see entities make the wrong choice. I want and often do see the good in creation, but how can I select the proper content without holy help? If I say discernment is from myself it is vain self-worship, and if I say it is from Him it's arrogant to the unbelieving world, to claim to be granted this ability. So there I am again: faced with content and choice and prayers for my sinful self to make the right ones and grow closer to Him. At last the doorknob stills and I know that I'm in peace again, though I wish I can say the same for the rest of them.

At dawn of the seventh day I go down to the living room, and all three of them are sitting there, glancing at me timidly, frazzled with red stains yet relieved.

Did you sleep well? asks the unharmed man.

Hard to say. And you? And they know I'm asking them all.

They chuckle in unison and though my reluctance hovers—taunting me to judge—a sense of understanding passes between us. Something happened—painting, writing, and mostly living and changing when facing demons—and no matter what it's called, things have shifted. The other man has a sprained wrist and seems unbothered by it, like he knows it could've been worse and would've found peace with that, too. The woman has decided to make an art piece inspired by the girl with no hands, a departure from her past work. So humbled that the devil can't take her—I almost say but don't. The unharmed man, who'd understood me from the beginning, suggests we all go for a walk for fresh air and chats with the neighbors, to which we all comply.

We got them, the lady neighbor with twinkling eyes whispers to me when I see her. *The ones who killed the other two. Their corpses are to be left out; a modern fairy tale sending its overdue lesson*, she smirks.

I smile back, comforted to be reminded of the strength of such patient townspeople. They are a law unto themselves, as it should be. In fact, it's really quite familiar, isn't it? Like a lovely secret abode in the dusty desert somewhere in the vast Middle East that some come back from, and some don't. Some things are understood across cultures, after all.

The others have decided to stay at the residence, at least for a while, a mix of guilt and duty calling for repentant work and growth. I don't tell them that the angry spirits of the dead still linger around—enduring lessons to be learned from both sides—though they'll probably find this out in due time. For the sake of political correctness and other more important pandemic and global matters, we're not shocked that the harrowing story will hardly get news coverage.

But for those who know how to look, the story not only exists but circulates in various forms, so my work here is done.

BEAUTIFUL DAY
IN PARIS

I almost can't believe I'm here, that I've returned, and so soon after... What did I expect? *La chaleur*—the fire to burst out of my veins, proving the fullness of life that was this place? Instead it's the chill, trying to freeze all things into helplessness—and this time, I'm the one to help handle the situation. Duty, you see. A *miles Christi* never gives up, especially not when you're blessed to know the true God.

I don't have time to waste, so I'll just say the obvious: that He has always been, and it's all culminated in the most important name: Yeshua. Some lazy parrots will think it's all the same, that they all lead to the "same but different" extremes—without even having read the texts! And that's where they prove yet again that they don't have the right discernment, though I hope in His name that will soon change. The thing with death is that it's everywhere and all too happy to catch you unaware—especially when you ignore or downplay it. Those who know can't pretend not to know, and when it's partially the laxity that has allowed all this to happen, over and over again like a repeatedly failed lesson.

All thanks to Him, there's always us—many, actually—to set the scales back where they belong. The Alpha and the Omega; people would know if they read, processed, feasted on and carved the holy texts into their heart's flesh. I keep thinking that they *pretend* not to know, so they can't really be surprised at the state of affairs. But sometimes I consider that they truly *don't* know. In that case, I'm too glad to remind them that the devil is a copycat.

How could I possibly die when I'm possessed by the source of life! Only fellow brothers and sisters in His service will understand how at peace I am, on this grey Parisian day. I get dressed and go on my favorite walk in my woolen hooded robes, pay respects to Archangel Michael at the fountain and go on to nearby Notre Dame. I was here then, too, *au Moyen Âge*, speechless as the stones piled up into twin towers, grazing the sky—and I could almost swear that if anything ever happens to her, I'd instantly toss the culprits into the perpetual flames they dismissed as nonexistent. But then again, it's often people who put themselves in it without anyone having to do a thing.

In the foggy dawn the serene quiet reigns as I circle around the glorious structure, heart filled with determination. Will it be *here*, will it be *there*? Will they finally change? But all the same: which the ideal place to do it? There are so many in Paris. We could say it's one long historical case of bursting creative energy, reflected everywhere—architecture, fashion, theater, food, music, nature—and I'm just one of the endless elements wallowing in it. Of course, it's not like I have to choose only one: the lesson will have to be sent from multiple points, after all.

I drift to the nearby Sainte Chapelle, the Conciergerie, the Louvre, the statue of Jeanne la Pucelle, with the same question lingering: where, where, where... And just like that, like so many things in life, the answer becomes so obvious: everywhere. The resolve makes me want to hurry to the glory—and in a sense, delay its human gratifying, too. Because if there's one thing I can't stand, it's how great humans can be at delaying the learning backed by consistent action.

At least, there's no denying that the difference is palpable from the previous time I was here—proof of at least some unspoken shift. While any such important bustling place would always have its tensions, it once had a stronger loving sense of self-preservation to counter, and sometimes even seduce it. Now the weight of chains hangs low in the air, ready to drop on too many masochists willing to accept it. That it has no power over me doesn't decrease my disgust mixed with sadness, always hoping to see that small yet distinct flash of yearning to elevate that is so painful but worth everything.

On I drift, the way I've done so often; history, memory, and reality merging into one eclectic mix. Most people don't see me and I'm fine with that. That's the difference between some of us: the boasting versus the humility. At times, when those possessed who know their time is up dare to look at me—reeking of vain challenge as if they could overcome me—they see me, headless, holding my own swarthy smiling head against my beating chest. And what's sad is that they can't stand it; this inability to get to you, that in a state that seems miserable to them isn't actually what it appears, and might even bring a solace they have yet to experience. Sometimes, worst of all to some is the concept that at last they might surrender, admit they've been lied to, and want to follow the true Light. Anything but that! The irony of free will, when they so rarely grant it.

And if it's just a harmless image, unable to touch them and their superior thinking, then why so upset? And in their fixation for such things, why are their own so consistently ugly?

The eye is the lamp of the body.

Yes, these days even those who thought they didn't care are being awakened, realizing in endless ways how different our visions are, the competing Masters that we serve. My favorite is when the better ones see me, bloody eyes gouged out and dark frazzled hair down to my muscular waist, and a soothing whisper envelops them—*Let me die with the Philistines!*

I continue my walk in the valley of the shadow of death: Montmartre, l'Opéra, l'Arc de Triomphe, Eiffel Tower, l'École Militaire, Champ de Mars, Luxembourg Gardens, la Seine—and the tour ends. My patience has worn thin too: how much evil can one allow before setting a line in the sand? Like any soldier knows, there's an ease to following orders, even if it's that selfish urge that might allow you to say, *I was just doing as told.* But that's in the event of error, which in His case is gloriously impossible.

Holy is His law: the balance will always be restored.

The time is at hand, so I pick my seat for the finale back at the Saint Michel fountain, with books, cafés, and the resonating human and water symphonies surrounding me. I relish the impending, overdue moment, as any of His servants would. It's not that sentimentality has gone—as if that is even possible—but rather that too much of it has played its part in the problem. And to think they had a Revolution with a regicide that claimed to favor reason over feeling! Men may be fickle—and forget-ful—but thankfully, many are gladly starting to see that He is not.

I stretch my arms wide up to the sky, hold in my breath and turn my knuckles into fists, and a torrent of shattering blasts echo everywhere. Near and far they thunder, from cafés, restaurants, venues, shops, and homes all over *la Cité des Lumières*. While the number of them varies by location, neither is any place completely free of them. A collective pause has set upon the entire witnessing Parisians, as they take in the outcome.

Here and there, monstrous heads lie blasted off, caused by the cell phone their hands still clutch—the fruit of their poisoned perception. On the screen, Telegram or other text messages apps are open, revealing their identity and reciting their evil intentions in their realtime voices. So many satanic plans that won't be boasted about, and will make others think twice about carrying out. The foul-smelling blood, strictly splattered on the guilty, and their hateful evil eyes and grotesque display does not inspire any sympathy. On the contrary, a collective sigh of relief washes over the survivors' faces, light and dark, local and foreign.

Then comes those demeanors—ranging from strangely blank to wildly shaken—that they almost look guilty of planning this event. But even through their disgust, the survivors are made to sense that their harmless phones are significant. Though some of the perplexed try to hide them, their phones suddenly light up and sing biblical verses they'd spent years, sometimes even a lifetime hiding from their intolerant, hateful communi-ties, often on pain of death.

Aside from being the most trustworthy narrator-witness, this is also part of where I come in—by helping to shed the veil between them to better see each other: they are safe, each from and with the other. At last, my hope is answered when gazes meet, confirming that from now on things will be different. In the pleasant stillness a bell rings three times and the criminal bodies, swallowed up by the judicious earth, vanish without a trace. Though it all somehow seems brief to them, they know it's no less intense and will not be forgotten. Thankfully it also serves to quickly reestablish the longed-for peace.

The devil is a copycat and feeds on tormenting the puppets who enable him. His deceived servants act because they're afraid, constantly threatened by someone else, even when their leader said and often proves that he can do nothing for them. We act because we're driven by His life-giving love and order. As He says, the truth shall set you free, and apparently humans can never be reminded too often. The truth is that we don't all serve the same God: if we did, we'd have the same goals of honoring His holy name in shared harmony, into eternity. At some point, we all have to choose.

The Lord comes like a thief in the night, and as His unworthy servant, I'll gratefully come along for the ride.

NEW CALIFORNIA

SAN FRANCISCO BAY AREA, POST 2020

If there's a calm before the storm, I relish the peace after it most. The once intimidating, deceitful monster with its limbs now splattered all over, the defeated evil gladly—and miraculously—swept away to make space for rightful, eternal order. The fresh unpolluted air and the blissful silence.

Oh, the silence.

The (surely temporarily?) impaired internet plays its part in that, and while I'm sure some are writhing in pain at this loss—not so much of real life as of fake identity—I've been enjoying it. Perhaps life is just an endless challenge in learning what to listen to, when the restless stirring voices never end. Maybe I don't want them to, and anyway it's not for me to decide on their existence either way. Still, I like to think I'm in charge of them with some indispensable holy help. How else could I even still be here to write this?

Here: in this blessedly preserved 20th century California Gothic mansion wrapped in eucalyptus trees. The doves coo sweetly nearby as I sip my Earl Grey tea somewhere in the early morning foggy Oakland hills. Occasionally there's a far-off lion's roar or a hyena's cackle, which is fitting, if only as a reminder of the wildness in and around us. Come to think of it,

I wonder if they'll rename at least some places around here; after everything that happened, it wouldn't be so surprising, and maybe even expected.

Even my name might eventually change, though I like being called BD. On the days when I don't think of myself as just cartoonishly existing after the deluge—am I alive, dead, or somewhere in between?—I'll recall that I'm a writer and possible actress, though sometimes I'm not sure there's a big difference between the two. While I wasn't born in California but was drawn here like many others, I've often thought that I love it as though I was, and despite my own conflicted feelings towards it across time.

Maybe that's what the recent cataclysmic earthquakes and flooding of the San Francisco Bay Area—that I was somehow meant to witness and survive—accomplished: they ironically removed my conflict to restore my cautious, yet unshakeable love of it. Strange, how so much can change but still feel *similar*... and even timeless in a way. Or is it that I've long been dwelling in my mind in the ideal version I had—have!—of this place? That thought amuses and satisfies me, because surely our lives are partially based on what fills our mind.

Perhaps it's the retrospect, but it's actually relaxing in a way, when on most mornings I relive that glorious day. I smile at William Keith's *Sunset on Mount Diablo* painting and as I stroll through the ample rooms of this lavish oak mansion with pointed arches, varied antiques and a vast library, the ground rumbles right from the earth's core, and the sky thunders in agreement. Steaming tea in hand, I love to float in that invisible cloud; savoring the simmering and gradual build-up that reminds me I wasn't alone in vomit-screaming from the pit of my stomach! Finally, the overdue blasting proof that I'd been heard all along, and even if I wasn't, there was glory in being able to humbly witness it, though I knew my earthly life could end at any moment.

Yet strangely, the more the ground shook and walls fell around me, nothing came close to harming me, so that I somehow knew how to navigate the elusive Big One that had been predicted for generations. Only that term is laughable now. There will never be words to fully capture the reckoning that unfolded, though what remains speaks for itself.

What happened is that most Bay Area homes were reduced to rubble, with people in and out of them. The earth split so decisively that it carved off the Castro neighborhood into an island and pushed it straight north into the Bay, west of Alcatraz. As unexpected as that was, I can't be the only to think that it's at least partially what some have always wanted, and are now served the sentence.

Following some divinely appointed decree, the Bay then narrowed, pulling the Golden Gate Bridge apart as the continent shifted east closer to Oakland. Biblical waters then surged and poured in so that it spared almost no terrain, flooding nearly the entire west side and into the East Bay all the way to MacArthur nearby.

I've been thinking of the Mountain View cemetery and all its bones pushed around by thick mud, mixing with putrefying corpses... Will I find Elizabeth Short and all the others? Surely she will tell me, just like the writing does. Would *anyone* take the time to check on me, too? I wonder then shake off the thought, knowing we all have our things and I don't expect it anyway. Still, maybe in time it would be nice to hear some news. One of these days I must go and have a look, armed with guns and cleaning materials to set things right as needed. I'd surely do the same for the dilapidated Oakland Zoo, though I'm sure by now none of the surviving animals that escaped are pining to get back into a cage. Amidst the lurking danger, if I had to choose I think I'd rather be killed by an animal than a human being—somehow it wouldn't feel as personal.

I turn on the radio, that classic potential source of news in times of disasters, and my soul rejoices at the sound of the perfect "Belaya Noch" by Chernikovskaya Hata. As another proof that God is ever merciful, one of the positive side effects of all this has been the introduction of some Russian songs into our decaying American culture, courtesy of President Putin who was the first to offer his generous aid in response to our plight. Anyone even remotely familiar with some basic history needs little reminder of past and present Russian cultural contributions, and I welcome such gems. After all, everyone is a little bit Russian when hearing Shaman's "Ya Russky." The gift of any art is to touch audiences and inspire empathy for others' experiences. Perhaps that's partly why I seek it out through writing and acting, as unpredictable or even painful as either may be.

And yet, it gets me thinking about the things that were spared, the areas that were less impacted. Like the Cliff House area where a struggling Rudy Valentino once gave dance lessons, or the Richmond district with its Holy Virgin Russian Orthodox Church. Then there's the Presidio park dating back to its roots as a 1776 Spanish military outpost first sited by Juan Bautista de Anza. And majestically overlooking the whole Bay Area from the East Bay is Mount Diablo, believed by several California Native Americans to be the point of creation.

Perhaps there's hope for me, too. I'm here, alive, in a spared beautiful home that seems meant for me, at least for the time being. Maybe Shirley Jackson and her architect ancestors would approve, or at least find some humor in it. I could do worse than be here so I'll enjoy every moment, and it occurs to me that maybe even Los Angeles is no longer the way I've imagined it. Isn't surviving good enough of a "big break"? Somehow for the first time I don't feel like I'm missing something, and I'm grateful for it.

We interrupt this broadcast to inform you that after weeks of disconnect, the internet is now restored. Unsurprisingly, Elon Musk has been one of the main donors to the ongoing relief effort, along with President Putin, and is surely glad to be back on X, as much to inform about this work as to share his particular brand of humor.

I wince, and not just because I've finished my tea.

I hear what's not said: that the lying American government can hardly be bothered to care for its own, while constantly printing money for other countries whose troubles it often stirred. Or that global nations can care—or pretend to—for international refugees without having to prioritize them to the recipient nation's detriment. Or that some health measure shouldn't be forced on some and not others, and other serious matters that are fodder for polarizing social media madness...

The internet was bound to come back but a part of me dreads all the noise that will inevitably follow from it—flooded timelines and users rushing in to "see" what's been going on, vague and graphic images of all the stuff they've missed out on. And then the draining, nagging need to share their own, as if actually *living* wasn't enough! Truth, lies, a mix of both... It's enough playing detective and sheriff stepping out the door, calculating the kind of justice and law I'll have to administer on whatever shifty entity I encounter—*This space is mine and I'll defend it!* It's human nature, or maybe savage nature but God did not give us life to never defend it. The nice thing is that by now I know good souls never want to intrude; so different from those yearning to latch onto and carve into you, split you into pieces for their twisted enjoyment.

More news just in! To be expected as we restore communication—chuckles the host. *In light of California's previous governor passing away, the unprecedented emergency vote count is in and an Independent is now in office. That's sure to be a change, even from the last Republican Terminator—er, I mean Arnold Schwarzenegger in 2011. After relief efforts, his next agenda item has yielded a death penalty law for all forms of human and child trafficking, and any violating activities connected with it. For those who haven't swarmed X yet, this measure is entirely supported by Elon Musk.*

Almost instantly, my cell phone goes off—that robotic thing I'd left on a beautifully aged oak counter, as if its screen reflecting every dust particle should be worthy of my constant attention. It's nice to hear from friends in a group chat, but then again, I like to think we were always communicating despite the circumstances.

Is this a joke? Seems too good to be true.
texts Sailor, from Port Chicago by way of Virginia and West Africa.
I concur, I reply.
The tides are finally turning,
replies Dancing Bear of Aleut and Russian heritage.
How long until some say it's Putin? I text.
Isn't it though?
winks Dancing Bear.
Or Elon—this talk tbc upon our immediate meet up.
smiles Sailor.

These loyal friends, kind souls coming to check on me and replenish me with ancient creation stories, so I'll prepare some rice with chicken and vegetables for lunch, then maybe go on a hike and see if the places and stories even match the media's. Sometimes it feels like a séance that never ends, and I like it that way. Truly it's another day to be alive—alone or not—and I'll take it one day at a time.

Then when I'm ready, I'll go to the cemetery, see people and animals and everything else for myself, chart a path and remap like my own De Anza expedition from the top of Mount Diablo. I used to be scared of change and though the fear still creeps in, I'm less afraid of being pulled apart and mended again.

ABOUT THE AUTHOR

Born in Brussels, Belgium, Natacha Pavlov is a bilingual Christian writer of German, Russian, and Christian Palestinian heritage.

A lifelong book and storytelling enthusiast, her novel *Jayida* (2023) is the fruit of years of research and the project that first made her want to write historical fiction. She is also the author of the historical fiction novel *The Well-Loved Demon* (2022) on the 18th century French King Louis XV, the novella *Nicola's Leg* (2017), and the short story collection *Twisted Reflections* (2015).

She is currently at work on more historical fiction.

Visit her at www.natachapavlov.com.